Show Me Good Land

SHONNA MILLIKEN HUMPHREY

Down East

This novel is a work of fiction. All characters appearing in this work are fictitious. Any resemblance to real individuals, living or dead, is purely coincidental.
While some of the landscapes and businesses may be actual places, or based on
actual places, the events portrayed in this novel and the actions of the characters
in these places are entirely fictitious.

Cover photographs © William Hubbell
and © Stephen Morris

ISBN: 978-0-89272-916-6

Designed by Lynda Chilton
Printed at Thomson Shore

5   4   3   2   1

BOOKS·MAGAZINE·ONLINE
www.downeast.com

Distributed to the trade by National Book Network

Library of Congress Cataloging-in-Publication Data

Humphrey, Shonna Milliken.
  Show me good land / Shonna Milliken Humphrey.
    p. cm.
  ISBN 978-0-89272-916-6 (trade hardcover : alk. paper)
  1. City and town life--Maine--Fiction. 2. Maine--Rural
conditions--Fiction. 3. Murder--Fiction. 4. Families--Fiction. 5. Loss
(Psychology)--Fiction. 6. Domestic fiction. 7. Psychological fiction. I.
Title.
  PS3608.U4745S49 2011
  813'.6--dc22

For Travis, my man

*B*etween the saline coastal swamps and the darkling forests of the interior, laid a northern route both treacherous and uncertain. Colonel Silas Angus marched bravely forward, with two men as survey crew. Presently, they came upon a naked savage standing in this foul path. The savage approached the drawn weapon of Colonel Angus without fear, and the good Colonel saw that Providence had sent this savage to him.

"Come," spoke the savage. "I will show you good land."

—*Excerpt of town history, engraved on a tarnished metal plaque, fixed to a lichen-covered slab of granite at the center of the crumbling Fort Angus garrison.*

1

ODIE HOLLANDER IN JAIL.

*W*hen Odie Hollander learned his mother was dead, he cocked his head, as if he hadn't quite heard the court-appointed lawyer's words. His acknowledgment came slow, like the thickest dirty motor oil, so the lawyer repeated herself. Odie affected a nod, but otherwise sat in the same sprawled position. His orange jumpsuit made a stark contrast to the gunmetal chair, his plastic sandals more so.

Even though it was only county lockup, the lightest of all possible incarceration, it was suicide to show emotion, so Odie stayed in the tiny processing room, boneless as a teenager and silent. Inside Odie's brain, however, the connections fired rapid. His mum had visited him just two nights ago. She was the one with the prescription idea.

"What would this sell for?" An aging Sheila Hollander had pushed the prescription papers across the wooden visitor table along with two cartons of hard-pack Camels, and for a man of limited education, Odie calculated the street value with an instant, audible "Holy shit." Odie's bail had been set for $10,000, and with his expletive, Sheila Hollander knew her plan was in motion.

‹◦›

It wasn't that Sheila Hollander condoned Odie landing Peg in the hospital with a split eardrum. Not at all. Odie was a big boy with a big temper, and in his six years with Peg Shane, Sheila reasoned, Peg should have known as much. Not that Odie shouldn't be responsible, but to Sheila's way of thinking, if the restraining order was on Odie, it meant Peg was supposed to stay away, too. So, when Peg showed up at Odie's place after she heard he'd left the bar with that girl who waited tables up at the truck stop, and then Odie smacked Peg off his porch for calling that girl a whore, it didn't seem fair that Odie was the one spending one hundred and twenty days in jail.

No, that didn't seem fair at all, and Officer Monroe would not have seen the meth supplies if he hadn't responded to that truck-stop girl's hysterical phone call and found Odie still punching Peg in the driveway. Plus, that truck-stop girl didn't have sense to hide the supplies away when she saw the blue lights coming down the road. In addition to Peg Shane, Sheila Hollander blamed the truck stop-girl, too.

Since this wasn't Odie's first offense, he didn't stand a chance in court, with his solid body sitting opposite Peg's tiny, bandaged frame. Peg stood up in front of the judge and said she changed her mind, but even that didn't matter.

The judge saw a bully, just a big, mean bully. There was no time in court for Sheila to present the little heart-shaped card Odie brought home for Mother's Day in the third grade. He'd pasted bits of white doily onto a red construction-paper heart and written "I love you" in black crayon. Sheila wanted to shove her card in front of the judge's face and demand, "Would a bully do that?"

Instead, she just folded the red paper and placed it back into her purse, behind the zippered pocket where she kept a twenty-dollar bill—just in case—and now the two precious prescription slips.

When the court-appointed lawyer left, and Odie was led back to his cell, he leaned his thick shoulders against the concrete wall and stretched his legs on the wool-covered cot. His cell was tiny, but there was a narrow Plexiglas window behind the steel toilet, and Odie watched the colors through the scratched plastic. It was twilight, and the setting sun cast dull orange shadows on the gray floor. His mother had been dead all day.

Odie's face remained expressionless, his features fixed and unyielding as he processed the information. His mother was dead, but he focused on the lawyer's other word: robbery. He thought back to who had been in the visitor's room when she came by with the prescription plan, who knew her address at Dupree's trailer park. As Odie leaned back against the wall, his memory relaxed and he tried to recall each detail.

In his mind, he scanned the visitor's room from left to right. He moved from the heavy metal double door across the cinderblocks painted a flat shade of green. The guard? No, he was a part-time town employee. He was bloated and lazy and wouldn't know what to do with that kind of stash.

Odie pictured the two long tables with rows of uneven and dented chairs on each side. His mother had visited him on a slow night, and the only other person in the room was somebody's girlfriend. Big tits, Odie remembered. The big-tit girl waited at a table until the guard said her boyfriend had spit in the clerk's face earlier that day and lost visiting privileges until further notice. Disgusted, the big-tit girl bounced out before either Odie or Sheila had a chance to talk details.

Two rusted electric fans were brought in to cut through the early August heat, but the fans just pushed the heavy air from side to side as they twisted and thumped. Odie sat alone at the table, and his mother tied her sweaty hair off her neck with a red bandana before reaching into her purse. The air from one of the fans lifted the edges of the bandana as they spoke, Odie remembered. When he recalled the industrial smell of the just-mopped floor tiles, laid unevenly in the farthest corner, it hit him. Hit him quick like a baseball bat.

Peg. Peg's brother Spick. S-Dawg, Odie called him at the Fourth of July barbeque, when things were good with Peg and she straddled his leg in the old plastic lawn chair while Spick tossed him beer after beer from the cooler.

"Fucking Spick," Odie said, unsure if it was out loud or not.

Spick fixed brakes and pumped gas at the machine shop for Odie's cousin Emmett. He also ran weed across the border for extra cash, and when he started cooking meth as a small-time batcher, Odie got in. Spick talked about scoring the cotton, saying that meth and weed were chump change. "Chump change" is exactly how he'd said it, and he gestured with his clammy little fist like he was some kind of city street rap gangster instead of a sickly white County boy from northern Maine. The cash, Spick told him, is in the cotton.

"Da cotton" he said again with the same pumping hand gesture, and Odie remembered wanting to punch the posing little fucker in his face.

Sheila Hollander knew she had about $10,000 of drugs in her purse when she left the Rite Aid, and though she never got high, she wondered about the pills. She wondered what sort of escape shot out of those tiny round tablets, and what it felt like to let go. She wondered if it was this kind of pill that made Odie switch from pot, the same pill that made the meth seem easy, like beer. Was it the pills or the meth that turned Odie's beautiful teeth yellow and rotten? Sheila was proud that in a classroom full of crooked smiles, Odie never needed to see a dentist. Not once.

"I'm going down to my sister's in Florida," she told Dr. Benis. "She's got the breast cancer, so I don't know when I'll be back." That part was mostly true. The stress of her son in jail and her sister's medical situation made her back hurt, this part was the lie. Bad, she emphasized.

Dr. Benis looked over his eyeglasses at Sheila Hollander with sympathy for her pinched nerves, as he suffered from one himself. When he wrote her a six-month prescription for two very powerful painkillers, she politely thanked him with sincere gratitude. That part was true, too.

She felt a tiny piece of regret for misleading the doctor, but this quickly eased. If Dr. Benis had paid any attention at all since he'd arrived in Fort Angus, he'd know the stress of a sick sister or an arrested son was nothing Sheila Hollander couldn't handle easily on her own. In her nearly seventy years, Sheila had seen much worse, more often, and she'd never needed any foolish doctor to offer medicine for something stupid as stress.

In fact, Sheila boasted, the only time she'd ever seen a doctor was when her two boys were born. Both surprises, one as a teenager and the second in mid-life, Sheila had been in and out of the hospital quickly. No drugs either.

While she was proud of this fact, she couldn't recall those two hospital visits without also remembering that her oldest son—Odie's brother Lamen, was still dead. He came back from Vietnam and then shot himself over a woman, Sheila remembered with bitterness, acutely aware that it was just her and Odie now. As a result, Sheila remained intent on keeping Odie safe. Sheila wondered if Dr. Benis had ever buried a child, and immediately doubted as much. Burying your child, that was stress.

Since Dr. Benis was dumb enough to believe the stress of a sick sister was worse than burying her own son, Sheila's guilt eased even more, and she drove her old station wagon home from the pharmacy with relaxed arms. It was, she figured, mostly the doctor's own fault.

Sheila telephoned Sam, Peg Shane's younger brother, the boy Odie called Spick, as soon as she'd filled the prescriptions. After Sam agreed to pay her the next morning, she made a second call to her grandson Jody-Ray to say good-night, but when Peg answered, Sheila hung up. Despite trying to get the charges taken away, Peg Shane was still on Sheila's shit list. Then Sheila Hollander turned off the kitchen light, locked the trailer door, and went to bed.

The court-appointed lawyer gave Odie minimal details, so all Odie knew was robbery. He knew dead. He knew no bail money now, so the full four months. And he knew Spick.

He remembered how Spick hovered over the old Styrofoam beer cooler just before the fireworks, all hopped up and squirrelly. Odie didn't like how Spick kept slapping Jody-Ray's head, laughing each time with his woodpecker laugh.

"Boy," Odie hollered at Jody-Ray that day. Just once, Odie remembered. He only had to holler at his son once. "Go on with your nana." He pointed toward the driveway and his mother's wood-sided station wagon idling in a puddle. Sheila was taking Jody-Ray and Peg's two girls to the fireworks, so Odie and Peg could go to the fair alone. Peg had played bingo in the tent that afternoon, won fifty dollars, and the two of them were hungry for fried dough.

The sun edged past the old farmhouse roofline, and Odie watched Jody-Ray run toward Sheila with orange Popsicle dripping down his arm. Peg's girls followed, walking with a lazy stride and swinging sparkly little pocketbooks. Before Odie could tell the oldest to scrape off the blue eye makeup, Peg asked if he wanted another burger from the grill. Odie turned to answer, and when he moved, Spick crossed his path, jumping Odie's nerves from the surprise of his sudden presence.

"Man, I gotta take a piss," he'd said, squinting under a ball cap turned sideways. That was the last time Odie saw Spick, when he was headed for the woods behind the house, his scrawny frame bent forward under that stupid ball cap.

Peg stood on the porch in her new white shorts while Jody-Ray waved from the front seat, and as soon as Sheila's car was out of sight, Peg was behind Odie, rubbing her hand against the front of his Levis. He remembered the metal screen door slamming shut as they walked upstairs, neither of them caring about Spick at that moment.

Then all the shit went down with Peg and that waitress, and now Odie sat on his little cot watching the sun through scratched plastic, smelling the dirty-feet smell of his jail cell with his mum dead. He rapped the back of his hand against his knee. "Fucking Spick."

The court-appointed lawyer made it so Odie could attend the funeral. Peg showed up at the jail with his clean jeans, an ironed blue shirt on a hanger, and the news that she was pregnant again. His Aunt Lora drove up from Tampa to set up arrangements, and together she and Peg cleaned out Sheila Hollander's trailer.

The two women picked over belongings and put them all in old grocery boxes labeled Keep or Trash. When Peg emptied Sheila's purse, she pocketed the twenty-dollar bill and tossed a tattered old valentine into the trash box. Peg and Lora clucked like chickens, asking each other over and over who could've done it and why.

"At least Jody-Ray don't have to see his daddy in handcuffs," Lora said as she handed the scowling reverend a check and nodded to Officer Monroe at the funeral. "And he'll be home by Christmas." Odie hadn't even thought of that part, the paying part, or the handcuffs, or the holidays, as Jody-Ray sat on his lap during the service, sucking a thumb.

Odie looked straight ahead at his mother's narrow white casket. The reverend's words were slow, and Odie watched sweat from the hot day make bigger and bigger wet circles under the man's armpits as he preached about Jesus and shepherds and still waters.

Peg sat on one side of Odie and Lora on the other, while Officer Monroe stood in uniform with a leather-gloved palm on his holster. Odie saw cousin Emmett, Lora's son, moving down the row of folding chairs. It occurred to Odie to whisper "Hey Emmett," but at that moment Peg grabbed his hand to pray.

When Sheila Hollander was cried over and buried, and Lora was handing the reverend a check, Odie went back to county lockup. Peg made her girls take Jody-Ray home so she could walk beside Odie to the squad car. He wanted to ask about her brother, Spick. Where he was. If she was in on any of it.

"So I'll come and see you on Sunday?" Peg reached up around Odie's neck as she kissed him good-bye. He nodded, smelling

Peg's lemon shampoo, but also wondering where Spick had taken off to, if he'd sold the pills, and where the money was. Most of all, Odie wanted to know what the fuck her brother was thinking. And again, if Peg was in on it.

He watched Peg's face as she drew back from his arms. When Peg lied, she never looked directly at Odie, her big blue eyes flicked left and the freckled skin on her nose wrinkled into lines. He watched her eyes look straight back at him all morning over a nose with skin stretched tight and even. Peg bunched her hair into an elastic band while she waited beside him, and he hoped more than anything Peg wasn't in on it.

Officer Monroe opened the squad-car door and told Peg that he'd solve the crime and bring the perpetrator to justice. "Perpetrator to justice" were his exact words. Monroe was from downstate.

Odie Hollander figured out who did it twenty-four hours after the crime was committed. That was the easy part. What he didn't know was the punishment. But, Odie reasoned, he had time. He had almost four months to work it all out, and right then, watching Peg stand with the rest of his family in the hot August graveyard through the rear window of the squad car, those four months were forever, and Odie Hollander began to feel a twinge of something like regret.

2

EMMETT PRATT IS SUSPECTED OF MURDER.

Because Emmett Pratt's mother, Lora, deeded him her trailer when she left town, and because the trailer shared a dirt lot with Sheila Hollander, Emmett Pratt was an immediate suspect in his Aunt Sheila's murder. Officer Monroe made Emmett late for the Irving station five mornings straight after it happened, turning up at the door and scratching notes on a pad with his chewed-up pencil. "Tell me again, son, where were you on the night of Sheila Hollander's salacious murder?"

Each day, the adjective changed. It was a ferocious murder, a wicked murder, and a grievous murder, too. Officer Monroe left out the grim and bloody details of the stab wounds covering Sheila's throat and chest, but he enunciated each syllable and infused each question with a mix of formality and fake Alabama twang. Emmett remembered the recent *Matlock* marathon on Channel 13 as he leaned against the doorframe and stood on his newly painted red steps.

No matter how many times Emmett looked straight at Officer Monroe and said that he'd been here at his own trailer, sleeping in his own bed, when his aunt was killed, the squad car still rolled into his driveway at 6:30 each morning.

"It's true," Lora Pratt said with her arms crossed in front of her one good breast and her wig, the red one, fixed tidy. She sent her son inside to fix Officer Monroe a cup of coffee that first day. "Emmett ain't the killing type." Secretly, Lora was pleased that at least one of her boys had kept a steady job for so long. "General manager," she bragged to her Florida friends.

Emmett told Officer Monroe that he heard Sheila Hollander's old station wagon rumble into the shared driveway sometime after supper on the second night of August. Emmett remembered this because he'd mentioned the rusted muffler to Sheila a few weeks before, specifically at the postponed Fourth of July fireworks. Sheila had pulled into the parking lot of the fairgrounds, loaded down with kids anxious for the Ferris wheel. At that exact moment, Emmett had seen the back of Rhetta Ballou's head, home on a visit and walking the midway with her grandmother in a wheelchair. He remembered cursing to himself that Sheila arrived before he could run up to Rhetta and say "Hey there, remember me?" Instead, Emmett stood by his aunt's rolled-down window and told her that by the sound of the muffler, a patch job wasn't going to do it. He heard Jody-Ray holler "Cousin Emmett, Cousin Emmett" over the ragged muffler until the engine shut off. Emmett remembered tossing a nearly full pack of Juicy Fruit from his shirt pocket to a bouncing Jody-Ray, telling him to share with Peg's girls. Then Emmett remembered saying to bring the car by the shop, and he'd ask Sam Shane to fix it for the cost of parts.

By the time he'd told Sheila to come into the shop, Rhetta Ballou and her grandmother had disappeared into the crowd. Emmett remembered that, too, but did not say as much out loud.

Emmett explained to Officer Monroe that a few weeks went by and Sheila never brought the car in. This, Emmett said again, was exactly why he was able to remember the sound of the rusted muffler outside his trailer on the night she died. The noise had woken Emmett from his spot on the couch, so he stretched his arms high over his head, stood up, scraped leftover macaroni and cheese from the pot into the dog bowl, rinsed his dirty plate, and turned off the kitchen light. His dog, a stocky yellow Labrador mutt named Lucy, licked Emmett's hand while he spoke.

Next, Emmett told Officer Monroe, he remembered checking the closet for a clean uniform shirt, and then he went to bed. Emmett woke up on the morning of August third, took a shower, dressed, drove to the Irving with his dog, clocked in, and when he got home that night, Officer Monroe and a bunch of state guys had taped off her half of the dooryard as a crime scene. That was, Emmett swore as he recounted the details each morning on his porch step, all he knew.

Since Sheila's youngest son Odie was in jail on a drug violation, and her oldest boy Lamen had killed himself many years ago, that left Emmett in the trailer park, and he called his mother long-distance when he heard.

·∾·

Lora Pratt was on the road for two days straight with her collection of wigs and spare boobs in the back seat, upset about her sister, but also wondering if she'd see her ex-husband Dexter's chickenshit face. Run off with that skinny mayor's wife, now that was low. Twentysome years later and ten states away, Lora still felt every pinch of that particular summer.

"Nasty blonde whore," she'd said to Sheila on the night Lora decided to carry Dexter's clothing by the armful from their shared closet, making a big pile in the Dupree Trailer Park entrance. She topped the pile with his special orange hunting jacket and then his ten years of *Penthouse* magazines dating back to before it was fashionable to wax all the hair off your crotch. Lora had paused briefly to note that her own tits looked just as round and tight as those in the colored centerfolds. In fact, Dexter had told her so again and again, right up to when he was arrested for leaving town in a stolen car with the mayor's wife.

Lora noted to her sister that Lyddy Compton was a sickly pale mouse of a woman, flat-chested, with no ass to speak of, but that she'd kick it just the same. "Dexter's, too," Lora said, pushing her husband's fishing rod closer to the center of the pile with her toe. Sheila, older than Lora, tried to talk reason with her baby sister, but it didn't work. A splash of kerosene and the same match she'd lit her cigarette with had a younger Hartley Monroe issuing Lora a citation for burning without a permit.

"Best forty bucks I ever spent," she told Sheila as she watched her husband's possessions melt in the fire.

◇

For the sake of his mother, Emmett was glad his father saw fit to stay away from the funeral. It was no secret that Emmett's brother Johnny took after Dexter, and Emmett was his mother's boy. Looking at Johnny was like looking into Dexter's mirror. Both tall and lanky, Johnny and Dexter shared the same lazy smile and the same dimples on the left side. Both men had eyes that tightened up in the corners, and from the back it was hard to tell father from son.

"Nope," Dexter said, "I can't deny my Johnny," as he looked suspiciously at Emmett. It was all said in fun, and Dexter would cuff Emmett's head as he spoke, but it was true. There was no denying Johnny Pratt was Dexter's son.

Emmett Pratt took after Lora's side. His shoulders did not hunch forward, he was a good four inches shorter than his father, and where Johnny had the dark wiry Pratt hair, Emmett's was soft and sand-colored like Lora's and Sheila's. None of their boys, Lora and Sheila both bragged as they grew up, had ever been to a dentist, but had the whitest and straightest teeth in town.

Sheila's was a small funeral, and Emmett wasn't sure what to make of that. His brother Johnny with Wendy Jo and their kids; cousin Odie on a bereavement release from jail with Peg, her girls, and Jody-Ray; more of Wendy Jo's Delfino and Ballou family; and then some other ladies from when Sheila worked up at the glove factory. Ada Ballou, but no Rhetta, Emmett noticed. All totaled, there were about two dozen people sitting on metal folding chairs behind the white coffin.

Emmett remembered way back when the body of Steve Angus was found, chopped up and buried under a woodshed. It was the same summer his father was arrested and his mother left town. Even as a teenager, Emmett Pratt had been impressed with the size of the funeral crowd. People who didn't even know Steve Angus turned out to pay respects. Rows of slow-moving cars backed up along Main Street, from the high school gymnasium, where they'd done the service, practically all the way to the Wintergreen Cemetery itself.

He wondered why it wasn't that way for his Aunt Sheila. Hers was a murder, just the same as Steve Angus. Hers was the first murder in Fort Angus since Steve Angus's more than twenty years ago, and his had been the first murder in the whole of Aroostook County for three decades before that.

Emmett thought about asking his mother when he drove her home after the service, but Lora Pratt was carefully blotting her eyes with a tissue. "It ain't right, Emmett," she sniffled as she adjusted her wig, now blonde and curly. "It just ain't right."

When they returned to the trailer park, Officer Monroe's squad car was parked in the driveway. Officer Monroe stepped from behind the corner of Sheila's now-empty home.

"So Emmett," Officer Monroe began.

3

RHETTA BALLOU MOVES HOME.

While Emmett Pratt spent the late-summer weeks in Fort Angus being questioned about his role in Sheila Hollander's murder, Rhetta Ballou had spent those same weeks unpacking in the southern part of the state.

Rhetta's tiny apartment was a second-floor corner walk-up above an Indian restaurant on the edge of Portland's Arts District. She'd rented the space with plenty of time to settle in before the university's next session, and when she toured the apartment, she saw the Henry Wadsworth Longfellow statue from her kitchen window and heard music from the tiny concert venue across the street. Cunningham's Rare Books was easily walkable, and Rhetta looked forward to getting lost among those dusty shelves.

After she signed a lease with the frog-eyed landlord, she had ordered takeout from the Indian restaurant. Rhetta's mother, Ada, called just as she picked up the bag of food.

Ada told Rhetta about Sheila Hollander's murder and how Hartley Monroe was looking at Emmett Pratt, and did she think she'd make it up in time for the funeral. "That would be nice," Ada mentioned with an edge in her tone.

Rhetta held the phone in the crook of her neck as she opened the door to her new apartment, and she sighed heavily into Ada's ear. Rhetta had just started her research job and could not take the time to attend the funeral. Rhetta spoke the words with a hint of apology, so Ada backed off. Ada said she understood. Work was work.

At 35, Rhetta spent her time on a graduate research fellowship for something Ada did not immediately understand. "You should go to school for computers," Ada told her again that day on the telephone. "Or, to be a nurse." Rhetta agreed those were both practical, smart ways to earn money, and then changed the subject.

She was just an Aroostook County girl back in Maine after nearly twenty years away, still disappointing her mother, but, she reflected when she hung up the telephone and rummaged to the bottom of a newspaper-filled packing box for a fork, she was also eating hot red curry in her own space. Things, she hoped, would be different.

Ada called again in late September, nearly two months after Sheila Hollander's murder, about cousin Wendy Jo, and this time Rhetta was on the road the next morning. She could avoid coming home for Sheila Hollander's funeral, but Wendy Jo was actual family.

Wendy Jo was placed in the intensive care unit at Fort Angus Regional Hospital for a methamphetamine detoxification regimen. The methamphetamine caused a severe kidney infection and while her cousin was not dead yet, it looked bad. Rhetta left messages for her professors and packed her car for the six-hour drive north.

The infection seeped into her bloodstream, and now Wendy Jo was all hooked up to the constantly beeping machines, her dirty blond hair framing a gaunt and unkempt face. At least, this is how Rhetta imagined it. Rhetta could clearly envision the hospital and its gray exterior. She saw the large revolving glass door and the long stretch of green shiny floor tile leading toward the intensive care wing. What Rhetta could not see clearly was Wendy Jo's face. Blond, she knew. Skinny too—rail thin, pale, haven't-eaten-in-a-week skinny.

The last time Rhetta saw Wendy Jo, she'd stopped in to Ada's house on the way to the postponed Fourth of July fireworks. Rhetta was in Maine to sort out moving details, and she'd driven north for a visit.

Wendy Jo's youngest daughter had to use the bathroom, and she walked her upstairs by the hand. Wendy Jo's older son was outside on the front porch, hollering to hurry up. Rhetta remembered Wendy Jo's bony shoulders, bony arms, and bony hands.

The cousins had nothing to say that day. Rhetta was shocked at the physical change in Wendy Jo, and for her part, Wendy Jo did not seem to even notice Rhetta sitting at Ada's kitchen table.

So when Ada told Rhetta the details of Wendy Jo's overdose that late September night, Rhetta tried to remember Wendy Jo's face, but all she could summon was the gaunt image of Wendy Jo slapping her son's head and telling him to shut up as they walked down Ada's hard dirt driveway.

Just after the fireworks, Wendy Jo moved out of the farmhouse she shared with her husband and the rest of her extended family, leaving the youngest kids with her mother, Ada's sister Christine, and she went to live by the river in an old shack with Sam Shane. Ada said Wendy Jo'd been high every day since.

Sam Shane ran guns across the Canadian border for money, Ada told her. Weed, too. And, Rhetta suspected when Ada described the rotten teeth, methamphetamine. Ada said Wendy Jo drove Sam's black Chevy through a stoplight and when she came back with a ticket from Hartley Monroe, Sam cracked her jaw with his fist.

As Ada told the story, Rhetta could not shake the image of Sam Shane himself. She could not imagine his chapped and scabby knuckles anywhere near her body, nor his yellow-toothed mouth on hers. Rhetta tried to imagine what he could offer any woman.

"Drugs," Ada repeated, bringing Rhetta back to the immediate conversation. "They are all on drugs."

Rhetta reminded Ada that they'd been doing drugs in some form for years. All of them. Christine and her husband Paul, even. Wendy Jo, and all the people in and out of their old Fort Angus farmhouse. Rhetta told Ada that if she were a social worker, she'd remove all the kids from that environment immediately. Like, today.

That was when the conversation with her mother had twisted, Rhetta recalled, struggling with one hand to peel back the flap on the coffee cup lid while she steered her car down outer Congress Street, over the railroad tracks, past the road to the correctional center, toward the ramp for I-295 northbound. After Ada detailed the rampant drug use for an hour, after going on and on about the safety of all those kids, Christine and Paul's age, the mental stability of all involved, how they were poorer than poor, and the necessity for someone to do something, she turned on Rhetta, saying she didn't know where Rhetta got off saying as much.

"Those kids are loved there. Christine and Paul are all they've got. Taking them away would be the worst thing for everybody."

Rhetta heard her mother's shallow breathing on the telephone, but she could not stop herself from responding. She pointed out that since they were children, they would be loved anywhere, that grandparents had very few guaranteed legal rights, and that it certainly was not the worst thing, but before Rhetta finished her sentence, there was an irreversible chill between them.

Ada told her not to forget where she came from, that she was no better than anybody else, and that she had best quit trying to put on airs. Rhetta sat quiet on the opposite end of the phone and took it. She marveled at Ada's quick turnaround from running down her cousins to running her down, but she took it, silent, all the time thinking that she didn't know which direction to move.

Rhetta was in a doorway, one foot on either side. She could join with her mother in the tirade, blaming this situation with Wendy Jo on the drugs and lack of drug enforcement. Blaming it on the area, the northern Maine economy, the lack of opportunity would buy Rhetta some validity, and for a moment, she'd feel a sense of belonging in that shared injustice of fate and place. Ada would relax her focus, content that her daughter was right there beside her.

Or, she could point out that Wendy Jo made some stupid choices, facilitated by her parents' stupid choices, and was likely to perpetuate stupid choices in her own children—that to break that cycle would be the kindest thing possible.

But by saying as much, Rhetta knew she was placing her own stupid choices somehow above Wendy Jo's. She'd be placing anyone's stupid choices above Wendy Jo's, and when it came down to it, dumb was dumb, with little distinction. Wendy Jo's stupid choices were no better or worse than any other person's, and Rhetta's own stupid choices stung her mind with amazing clarity.

Rhetta Ballou left Fort Angus when she was still a teenager, straight off an affair with a married teacher and an abortion nobody knew about. With a high school equivalency certificate and a brand new driver's license, Rhetta just pointed her beat up Chevy south and pushed the gas pedal hard.

"Get out of this town," Ada told her daughter over and over, almost every day as she grew up. "Get out of this town," she'd said. "Don't be like me," but Ada was still shocked when Rhetta left Fort Angus.

Leaving, Rhetta often thought, leaving home was the easy part. As Rhetta tried to walk a middle line with her mother on the telephone, she knew the hardest part was figuring out a way back.

"I'll be there tomorrow," she said, hanging up with a hollow click.

In the twenty years since Rhetta left Fort Angus, she'd acquired two graduate degrees and moved through twelve states. She was now headlong into a research fellowship that made no sense to her family.

"Rhetta must be the smartest woman in the world," Ada had said during the recent Fourth of July visit. "She's been going to school long enough."

Rhetta ignored the comment at the time, but her grand-mother, Nellie, out from the nursing home, snorted. When Ada spoke the words, Rhetta winced at Nellie's laugh.

Rhetta pushed that memory from her mind as she drove into the early-morning sun toward home. Twenty minutes up the highway, she passed the Freeport signs advertising L.L. Bean and the outlet shops, and she relaxed into her seat as she pondered the next six hours.

Fort Angus is a speck on the map. Printed in the tiniest font at the end of I-95, and then thirty miles north from the exact spot where the state becomes Canada, Fort Angus is part of a handful of towns and townships scattered throughout Aroostook County.

Fort Angus, the largest town in Aroostook County, the larg-est county east of the Mississippi River, was her hometown. She'd taken to calling Aroostook, "The County," but it never felt right, like something a person from away would say. Rhetta thought about Aroostook, its geographic remoteness, and of leaving her family who still lived there.

She put last night's conversation with her mother out of her mind, and tried to summon clearer, better, and more positive images of her cousin Wendy Jo. She wanted a sense of the cousin she had left, and the first memory was easy.

Ada used to drop Rhetta off at her sister Christine's house, just on the edge of Fort Angus—a rambling farmhouse inherited from the Delfino in-laws—a structure that had potential once, but now inspired very little in its current state of haggard yellow chippedness. Christine had eight children before she was twenty-three. At age fifteen, with her mother Nellie's endorsement, she had married a logger named Paul Delfino. "He don't beat you, and he makes good money," Nellie'd said.

Ada said her sister let her kids run wild, but young Rhetta thought her aunt was hip and fancy. Christine sold Avon from shiny square catalogs, and Rhetta practiced wearing the pink and red lipstick samples with Wendy Jo.

Nothing was off-limits at Christine's. There were no sheets on the bed, no need for a peanut butter knife when you had a finger, and sometimes Uncle Paul came home at lunchtime to make whoopee with Christine behind a closed bedroom door. Whoopee day or not, Rhetta and the cousins climbed onto countertops, drank straight from pitchers, and raced in stocking feet across the torn kitchen linoleum.

Christine's place had huge overgrown potato fields with a decrepit shell of a farm truck and an equally decrepit tractor, both prime places for hide and seek. Once, Wendy Jo and Rhetta made a secret clubhouse on the remains of the truck's flatbed. Wendy Jo said a garter snake ran over her toes the week before while she was wearing sandals, and that her dad had to beat the new dog when he wouldn't stop barking the night before.

"It's the only thing they understand," Wendy said. Rhetta nodded like she too understood, and then the two cousins threw a battery of choke cherries at Wendy Jo's little brothers and some other farm kids until they cried and ran inside to tell.

Christine's dusty stereo played country and western songs, and Rhetta and Wendy Jo used rolled up pieces of paper for microphones, learning all the words to every lonely, cheating ballad ever made popular by northern radio.

Christine inspected mosquito bites from her kitchen table, loaded down with magazine flyers, drawings, paper plates, and an open bag of potato chips. She drank Allen's coffee brandy with the lady who lived across the road and talked about dirty things, saying "partied too hard" and "honky-tonk whore."

Sometimes, if they all were good and could settle down and get out of her hair for five minutes, Christine would load the entire group into the old green Pontiac and drive to the quarry swimming hole near the north edge of the Abnaki River. It was before seat belt laws and all the kids clamored into the car, some standing on the floor and gripping the head rests, trying not to fall and injure those piled on the back seat.

Christine would pour her coffee brandy into an old Pepsi bottle, top it with milk, and find a *True Confessions* magazine. She'd sit herself at the edge of the water, adjust her bikini bottom while she rubbed Johnson's baby oil with iodine onto both legs, and warn about bloodsuckers. "I'm putting the salt shaker right here, so don't knock it into the water."

Then there was a tangled, wet mass of muddy kids. Splashing, the older ones tried not to hurt the babies. The big cousins told stories of old Leander Lambert's creepy river shack in the woods, and the little kids kicked and screamed and splashed away even faster.

It got cold at the end of the day, goosebumps eventually driving Rhetta and Wendy Jo in a barefoot clammy trek back to the Pontiac. There were only two thin orange towels to share, but Christine promised grilled cheese and baloney sandwiches if they all could shut up, and as a little girl holding hands with her best friend and favorite cousin, Rhetta couldn't imagine anything that tasted better or any day that could be more perfect.

That was the first of two images in Rhetta's mind when she remembered Wendy Jo. Grilled cheese, secret clubs, and a granite swimming hole in the cold Abnaki River. Passing the Brunswick exit, Rhetta shifted in the car seat and shrugged her shoulder muscles, happy with that memory. She and Wendy Jo had been friends as little girls, sharing a sleepover bed and running fast through overgrown potato ruts. The second biggest memory of

Wendy Jo was Aunt Joyce's wedding reception, and Rhetta loved this one, too.

When shy Drew Freid convinced the third and youngest Ballou sister, Joyce, to make it legal, it was the first Ballou family wedding in memory that didn't happen in the courthouse right before a new baby.

Drew Freid and Joyce Ballou got married the summer of the Steve Angus murder trial, Rhetta remembered, counting backward in her head and tapping years with her fingers on the steering wheel—it was two decades before Sheila Hollander would turn up dead. Liquored up and feeling brave, shy Drew Freid in his rented tuxedo had taken the microphone from the hired singer.

"I married a Ballou girl!" he shouted, and the crowd of his logging buddies cheered him with beer bottles held high. The rows of loud men turned out in their clean jeans and ironed shirts made Drew even more bold. He grabbed Joyce by the waist and twirled her around so the skirt of her wedding dress flew up to show the shiny white satin shoes underneath. Then he planted the biggest, wettest kiss on Joyce's mouth.

Joyce reached up, held his face and kissed him right back. That kiss and the way Joyce's lace dress looked so delicate in Drew's big calloused hands made everyone in the Ballou family feel good, like the youngest Ballou sister would be taken care of. Ada and Christine unwrapped fresh platters of ham salad sandwiches, while Nellie sat at the far end of the head table, cackling happy as Rhetta ran back and forth, refilling plastic cups.

Wendy Jo pinched Rhetta's elbow and handed her one of the ham salad sandwiches just as Joyce and Drew began to slow dance. The lights went low, and the two girls left through the side door of the Elks Club hall in their pink junior bridesmaid dresses while all the women in the room took the wrists of their men and tugged them away from the cash bar before the song ended.

"I want to show you something," Wendy Jo said, and Rhetta followed her thin ponytail into the fresh air. She could tell by the way her ponytail bounced that Wendy Jo had something fun in mind.

Wendy Jo had inherited the scrub-nosed Ballou grin from her mother, Christine, but her hair hung blond and limp just like her daddy, Paul Delfino. Rhetta's hair was bright red like her mother Ada's, passed straight through the Ballou line from Nellie. They walked down the steep concrete stairs onto Main Street.

The street itself was empty, and their stiff dress shoes made a hollow clompy sound on the sidewalk as they crossed to the library park. It was late into a summer night, but the moon hung so bright it could have been twilight. Rhetta remembered licking the last bit of ham salad from her thumb when she saw two figures on the park bench ahead.

Wendy Jo waved at the figures, and they stood up. It was Johnny Pratt and his brother, Emmett. The Pratts lived at the trailer park at the end of the Hope Station turnout, an offshoot of the old Garrison Hill Road, down a long dirt path that flooded after thunderstorms and got blocked in during snowstorms. The Pratts wore tight, white T-shirts and ripped jeans and carried sharp little knives in their jacket pockets. Until just recently, the two Pratt boys lived with their mother, Lora, while their father, Dexter, was in jail for stealing Mayor Compton's new Buick.

The way everyone heard it, Mayor Compton would've forgiven the car theft if his wife Lyddy hadn't been in the car with Dexter Pratt. Of course, Lyddy Compton said it was all Dexter's idea and that she'd been kidnapped, and even though Lyddy's yellow overnight bag was packed in the trunk beside Dexter's grease-stained duffel, all the mayor saw were his wife's teary brown eyes. Lyddy Compton came back home and, six months later, she gave birth to a skinny, dark-haired boy named Miles who looked nothing like her people or Mayor Compton's. Dexter Pratt went to jail, and two weeks later, Lora Pratt got fed up with it all and drove south to Florida, leaving her boys to fend for themselves.

Now, some twenty years later, Rhetta was surprised at the level of detail she could remember. The long interstate stretched gray and tight between the pines and stands of white birch, and she let her mind work its way back to the details of that summer night. She didn't know it at the time, but it was the last full summer she'd spend in Fort Angus.

Rhetta returned to Fort Angus for short visits and holidays, but during those short visits home there was never any time to get melancholy or sentimental. Rhetta drove up, ate Ada's home cooking, visited Nellie in the nursing home, and then pleaded airline schedules, a meeting time, or a new job, leaving as soon as the dynamic threatened to move past anything superficial.

Given that Rhetta was officially living in-state now, and this was her second trip home in a single season, she figured her memory must be expanding, so she eased even more into the details of the wedding reception.

There were the Pratt boys in the library park on the night of Joyce Ballou's wedding. Johnny's leg was propped up on the bench, Emmett sat straight, his hands in his jeans pockets.

"Hot damn, Wendy Jo," Johnny whistled, opening his arms wide in a gesture of excitement.

Rhetta was going to mimic Johnny's flat whistle and fake swoon, and then maybe get Wendy Jo to make fun of it, too, but when Rhetta looked sideways, she saw her cousin running hard at Johnny Pratt.

He picked her up and swung her around, not unlike the way Drew Freid had swung Joyce around the dance floor. Johnny swung her so hard she pitched a shoe. It flew over Emmett's head and hit a tree, landing softly in the grass. Rhetta moved to get it, and when she stood up with the shoe in hand, she no longer saw Wendy Jo.

Despite the moonlight, her scan found nothing but Emmett Pratt, still sitting on the park bench. He nodded toward the shadow of the old war monument, and she saw two vague figures huddled at its base. Rhetta turned back toward Emmett, and he grinned. Emmett had the nicest smile she'd seen on any boy. Johnny Pratt was eighteen, which made Emmett fifteen or sixteen—just about Rhetta's age. She heard muffled giggles from the shadows.

Rhetta shifted her legs and looked over her shoulder toward the Elks Club hall. She crossed her arms, feeling both ditched and duped by her cousin. She could not return to the reception without Wendy Jo, and she had no desire to wait on the park bench, listening to faint giggles from behind the war memorial.

"Want to go for a walk?" Emmett Pratt blurted, and she considered his offer for a moment before nodding, embarrassed, but grateful for something to do.

She didn't ask Emmett any questions, even though she wanted to know if it was hard living in a trailer alone with just his brother for company, and why he decided to quit school and work at the Irving station. Rhetta knew he worked there full-time because Ada filled up at the Irving and said Emmett was decent, especially given that his father was in jail and his mother'd just run off the way she did. Not that Ada blamed Lora for leaving Dexter Pratt. Ada would have done the same thing, she said. It was the boys being left that made her sad.

Rhetta and Emmett were silent as they walked down Main Street. The sound of the wedding reception, all pounding bass and loud laughter, moved with them for two full blocks—past the tall brick courthouse where Winona Peletier was on trial for killing Steve Angus, the smaller and newly constructed county jail where

Emmett's dad was spending two years for car theft and kidnapping, and all the way to the old clock tower. They walked farther toward the newspaper office next to the Hair Palace beauty salon, where Emmett's mother worked before she left town.

Each building they passed was connected to their collective history, and in deference, neither Emmett nor Rhetta spoke. They passed the Salvation Army that stood next to the Full Gospel Assembly, which was beside Bob Egler's electronics shop. The Sunrise Cinema marquee was lit up, and Rhetta knew the second showing would start soon. When they reached the stone statue erected in honor of the DAR ladies, Rhetta and Emmett turned around.

They made an odd pair, Rhetta Ballou walking barefoot and cross-armed in a long pink formal gown, while Emmett Pratt carried one of her blister-making shoes in each hand, both of them silent. For a Saturday night, Fort Angus was still. A few cars parked in the municipal lot with stereos thumping, and Emmett nodded at one of his brother's buddies leaning on the bumper of an old Monte Carlo, tipping a silver can of beer in the glow of the theater marquee.

Emmett Pratt and Rhetta Ballou traced their town like its earliest surveyors, moving past each landmark as casually as if they owned it all. The two walked the length of the hill, past the dairy bar and toward the old garrison. As they walked, Rhetta let her bare arm lean into Emmett's own bare arm. She leaned in just enough to feel his warm skin, and when she did, Emmett immediately straightened. He righted his posture, wondering if Rhetta

Ballou meant to touch him with her arm, and then figuring, no. No, she didn't. At least, not on purpose.

Rhetta did not speak, but she watched Emmett with quick, narrow glances. He walked on her left side during the trek up the hill and her opposite side for the return down, making sure to always put himself closest to the road. Even as a teen, Rhetta recognized the gesture as that of a gentleman.

Wendy Jo and Johnny Pratt were sitting on the library park bench when Rhetta and Emmett arrived after their walk. They were holding hands and passing a wrinkled joint between them. Wendy Jo's face was tipped up toward Johnny's, and she wore his oil-stained denim jacket over her pink dress. So it was no surprise to Rhetta when Christine and Paul Delfino signed the papers for Johnny Pratt to marry their expectant daughter in the courthouse four months later.

This, Rhetta thought at the beginning of her long drive home, was how she wanted to remember her cousin. Trying on lipstick samples and, later, falling into something like love—not laid up all trashy and close to death in a rural hospital.

As she drove, thinking back to Joyce's wedding night so long ago, it also occurred to her that the last and brightest remembrance of her cousin and childhood friend was not a memory of Wendy Jo at all, but a detailed image of Emmett Pratt.

4

Miles Compton returns home, too.

*O*n the other side of Fort Angus, far away from Emmett Pratt's trailer park, in the rows of orderly split-levels with neat front lawns, Miles Compton woke up in a twin bed across the hall from his father and wished for death. His father's, or his own. Maybe not a violent and gruesome death, with knives and supposed decapitation like Sheila Hollander's, but something smooth and quick. Something with dignity and possibly poise. Miles thought about the differences between good and bad death from his position under the old maroon sleeping bag, unzipped and spread to make a comforter.

He saw that it was a sunny blue August day around the edges of the window shade, but he was in no hurry to rise or to let any more light into his room. He enjoyed the vaguely cave-like atmosphere, and stretched from his left side to his right while wondering how quickly a bullet could kill a person and, more importantly, how bad it would hurt.

Miles heard his mother moving downstairs, heard the kitchen door open, heard her drag something heavy across the floor, then heard a bag of potatoes tumble into the cabinet bin. He heard the coffee maker gurgle, and when he heard the telephone ring, he knew he would soon hear the start of some fresh misery.

"Get your facts straight," Lyddy Compton said in a measured, practiced tone just before Miles heard the phone slam down. He thought he heard the small click of the telephone cord being pulled from the outlet, too.

Miles burrowed deeper into the sleeping bag, covering his head and shutting out even the small glints of sun from the edges of the shade. Lyddy Compton's straight facts were these: while Miles was studying at Bowdoin College, he interned without incident for a semester at a private boy's school in northern New Hampshire—without incident, until he fell in love with a slightly underage student. They carried on for the full semester until the boy's parents got Miles fired and publicly branded a sexual predator before he was even twenty-one years old.

"You must cease contact," the headmaster told him, peering over rimless eyeglasses and snapping a manila folder shut. Miles had never in his young life sat opposite a principal's desk for disciplinary action, and the sensation was foreign but exciting. His hard plastic seat made him shift with discomfort, and he remembered the bad boys at Fort Angus High School, a Delfino or a Pratt or a Shane leaning against the wall with fists shoved into old denim jackets and their boots or sneakers dirty from mud. Despite the serious nature of the conversation, Miles let his slight, clean body tingle at the memory of those gorgeous Fort Angus bad boys.

Miles heard the headmaster's words, nodded, and signed the

forms required for the protection order, but two days later in a fit of what he considered passion and his mother called stress, he was outside the junior dormitory. Miles had tracked this particular boy's trip home for the weekend, and watched him step off the returning bus just outside the school walls. He watched the boy heft his backpack and carry a paper sack (leftovers?) through the tall iron gates and up the manicured academy walkway. Because it was dinnertime, the quad was empty. When the boy reached his dormitory, a sobbing Miles moved from behind his tree and made himself known. An hour later, Miles was arrested, pleading that he just wanted to talk.

Stripped of his college enrollment and with his photo now up on the state website, Miles was acutely aware of his limited options, so when his mother called with the news of his father's advancing dementia, he agreed to help.

"Since Phil is busy with his family, I was hoping you could come home for a little while." These were her words, and Miles felt an ache of longing followed by a moment of suspicion. On the one hand, Miles had not been back to northern Maine for more than a Christmas holiday since he left for school. On the other hand, he was lonely. The idea of home, any home, appealed to him. That he was second choice to his older brother Phil did not surprise him.

Miles heard his father moving across the hall, and fearing a repeat of last week's toilet confusion, he rose to assist.

"This meeting will now come to order!" When Miles opened the bedroom door, he saw his father standing naked with a shampoo bottle in his hand, looking in vain for a gavel pad.

"Mayor Compton," Miles knew the drill. "Mayor Compton, may I help you?" He placed his hand gently on his father's fat back and led him to the bathroom.

Downstairs, Lyddy Compton poured a second cup. Since it was Wednesday, and the little Shane boy had delivered the *Fort Angus Republican* early, Lyddy read her paper. She scanned the headlines first. Sheila Hollander was still big news. Her obituary had run right after the murder, and the follow-up stories included a few grim photos of her cluttered bedroom where that poor little paper boy found her all twisted up. Like everyone else in town, Lyddy wondered who could have done such a horrible thing.

She suspected Emmett Pratt, but she could not articulate a reason. If she were a woman with self-awareness, she would know that she suspected Emmett Pratt because the whole of Fort Angus suspected Emmett Pratt. As it was, when Lyddy tried to articulate a justification, she kept returning to Emmett Pratt's dirty fingernails. Try as she might, and she did not try mightily, Lyddy could not grasp how any person could stand to be dirty. Soap was cheap, and in her mind, there was just no excuse, so when Emmett Pratt pumped her gas at the Irving station, and Lyddy had to pass money into his oil-stained hands, she shuddered, knowing those same hands had killed Sheila Hollander.

Teeth, too. Lyddy did not understand how a person could live with crooked, rotten teeth. That, she told her friend Karen

Angus, was why health insurance was invented: to fix dirty teeth. Her own husband's policy covered two dentist visits a year for everyone in her family, and in Lyddy's mind it made no sense for people like the Pratts not to make that appointment. Laziness was the only excuse she could assign, even though, when Lyddy thought about it, Emmett's teeth weren't all that bad. In fact, as Lyddy studied the blurry photograph in the newspaper, he very much resembled his father, Dexter, in that regard. Tall and thin, curly hair, Emmett was walking out the courthouse door beside Hartley Monroe when the picture was taken: Emmett Pratt, 35, person of interest.

With one hand in his pocket and the other carrying what looked like a stack of papers, Lyddy couldn't inspect his fingernails up close. Emmett still wore his Irving uniform, too, and she wondered why he hadn't changed into a suit for a court appearance. That showed disrespect in Lyddy's mind, and that level of disrespect for a public institution made her even more convinced that Emmett was the killer.

Still, though, it was a shame. Lyddy remembered the summer when his father, Dexter Pratt, seduced her by standing all lanky and grinning outside the movie theater. There'd been a murder trial that summer, too.

When Lyddy walked to the municipal parking lot on that particular evening with her brand-new car keys in hand, Dexter let out a long, slow whistle. She'd just finished with the evening church service, and planned to stop for a milkshake before driving home.

When Dexter whistled at her, she realized at that moment that no man had ever whistled after her in her entire life. She remembered checking the top buttons on her yellow dress, bought special for the social hour celebrating her birthday. Since all the buttons were pulled shut, she glanced down to see if her slip was hanging.

Even though she'd never been whistled at before, she had the sense to keep walking. She had sense, Lyddy remembered, until she turned around. It was a hot night, too hot for the season, and Dexter Pratt was shirtless in the municipal parking lot, drinking from a paper-wrapped bottle and leaning against the brick side of the Sunrise Cinema. He grinned again. Lyddy remembered his dimples and soft smile, so out of place on his hard, angular body.

And then, in some fit of craziness, Lyddy found herself smiling back. When Dexter gestured, she moved toward him, and she said yes when he offered to share his drink. She suspected it was drugged, and that's exactly what she told her husband when he slapped her face and demanded details.

Lyddy did not like to recall that unpleasant summer twenty years ago, so she focused again on the newspaper. Beyond the Sheila Hollander murder, there was general court news, wedding and birth notices, and the community-talk section. She searched for the announcement she placed wishing Phil and Rosemary a happy anniversary, and when she found it, she stood up to get the scissors from the drawer. She turned when she heard Miles moving behind her. He had dressed his father in tight, gray biking shorts and a loud, red floral Hawaiian shirt.

"He insisted," Miles offered. "We're in the islands today."

Lyddy sat back down.

Her husband's dementia diagnosis came the day after the Fourth of July fireworks. The fireworks had been postponed to Sunday night because of rain, and on Monday morning a yawning Dr. Benis gave them the news.

Lyddy remembered thinking she should reach for her husband's arm, but instead she sat in the wooden chair with her hands folded neatly on her lap while Dr. Benis spoke. Mayor Compton's brain could decline slowly, or it could go fast, but either way, it was going to happen.

Mayor Compton took the news well, slapping Dr. Benis on the arm before he left, not unlike a campaigning politician. While her husband tried to schedule a golf time with the doctor's secretary, Lyddy accepted a small stack of brochures from Dr. Benis and quietly thanked him.

The brochures had remained stuck in the drink holder of her old Buick for at least two weeks. They detailed the two Fort Angus nursing home options, with instructions on Medicare coverage and Social Security benefits.

Fortunately, Mayor Compton had dropped his legal practice down to part-time already, and Phil had taken on his father's clients for the duration of the mayoral term. "This is the last year, boys," Mayor Compton said each year his name was put forward by the council as a nominee.

The dementia was too much for Lyddy to process, and when she called her son Phil for advice, he let the phone ring and ring. Ever since getting that caller ID feature, Lyddy noticed that Phil and Rosemary seemed to be away every time she telephoned. Three times out of five, when she drove the four miles across town and down the Plantation Road to their new log home, the shades were drawn and the house was locked up, even the back door.

Lyddy had let the old Buick idle in their driveway on the afternoon of the diagnosis, and she wondered where the two of them could be, given that she knew Phil had taken the day off from work. There were no cars in the garage, and Karen Angus, Rosemary's mother, was not picking up her telephone either. Lyddy had a strong suspicion that she was being excluded from something fun.

"Dad's fine," Phil told her when she eventually reached him at the office the next morning. "He's just fine."

That left Miles. When Lyddy called him in New Hampshire to help pack the mayor off to the nursing home, she had no idea about his arrest. She learned about it from Karen Angus after church, when the entire Fort Angus Imperial Baptist Sanctuary congregation had been openly invited to pray for his gay sins and troubles. Karen Angus pulled her outside the back door of the church kitchen.

"I'm so sorry," Karen said as she crushed the lit end of her cigarette against the door jam and—because she was such a good friend, she insisted—told Lyddy that Miles was registered with a photo on the state pervert website. Karen Angus told Lyddy all this while making a big show of hugging her tightly.

Since Karen was Phil's mother-in-law, Lyddy needed to keep the peace, and keeping the peace is what Lyddy thought about while she was being hugged so hard the metal clip on her bra strap cut a tiny red mark into her back. She stood with her arms dangling, taking the hug and keeping the peace, wondering if the stories Karen was telling her about Miles were true.

It had been a long stretch of weeks since then, and now, as Lyddy drank her coffee and read her newspaper while Miles wrestled her husband into the kitchen chair for breakfast, she also wondered if Karen Angus would blame her for deciding to place the mayor into a nursing home. Karen would either blame her for driving the mayor crazy, or she'd be starting up a prayer circle, and at the moment Lyddy Compton could not decide which was worse.

5

Emmett Pratt thinks about his bank statements and Rhetta Ballou.

*W*hen Sheila Hollander's body was discovered by the paper boy, Officer Hartley Monroe had just arrived at the station, planning on a quick shower in the locker room and then a ride to the new Tim Horton's for coffee. Just before he got the call, Officer Monroe nodded to Joyce Freid at the reception desk as he punched into the ancient metal time clock. There was talk of switching over to a computer system, but that was just talk for now, and it would remain just talk if Officer Monroe had anything to say about it. You could cheat with a computer, but there was no frigging around with an ink stamp direct from the time clock itself. Officer Monroe stamped his own card with the heavy red lever, and he smiled with the machine's satisfying clunk.

With his uniform on a hanger and his shoes in an old backpack, Officer Monroe walked across the paneled waiting room in his sweatpants. From behind the plastic window, he watched Joyce Freid pick up the beige phone on the non-emergency line with her left hand as she stood to reach a file drawer with her right. Joyce Freid, Officer Monroe thought, is a good woman.

He watched Joyce's legs, wrapped in a pretty flowered skirt, move from the cabinet to the desk, and he was pleased that one of the Ballou girls finally made something of herself.

Officer Monroe's thoughts shifted from Joyce's braided red hair to how the Freid family were good, solid, decent country people, and he was just about to move back to thinking about Joyce's body again when he saw her hand move to her mouth as she sat down hard.

"Hartley, come here, quick," Joyce whispered as she extended the receiver. "You're going to want to take this one."

Since Emmett Pratt lived next door to Sheila Hollander, and since Emmett Pratt had no one to verify his whereabouts at the time of the murder, Officer Monroe was leaning heavily on the fact that Emmett Pratt had killed his aunt. While the state crew got more and more involved with the crime scene itself, Officer Monroe focused solely on Emmett. Eventually, he'd crack. Officer Monroe believed this, and he made a special point of questioning Emmett Pratt on his doorstep each morning, seizing upon little inconsistencies.

Once, Emmett said he went to bed. The next time? Emmett said he fell asleep. Which was it, Officer Monroe pressed, flipping through the pages of his narrow notepad. Did he go to bed or did he fall asleep? Whereas his secretary, Joyce Ballou, now Freid, came from trash, Emmett Pratt, in Officer Monroe's estimation as he stood in the dirt dooryard of the aluminum-sided trailer, would remain trash.

·〰·

Emmett Pratt just stopped going, that was how he quit school. When the Irving gas station manager heard that Dexter was going to jail for stealing the mayor's car and wife, and Lora had run off from the shame of it all, he offered Emmett a bump up to full-time with earned vacation and health insurance after ninety days. Emmett was barely sixteen, but he shook the manager's hand firmly and took the hours. Since then, every morning at seven he turned up to the shop in a clean shirt, ready to pump gas or change oil. His first paychecks showed thirty cents an hour over minimum wage each week, and Emmett felt rich.

A dime on every dollar went into the Maxwell House can on top of the refrigerator. That was his mother's long-distance advice. When the coffee can filled up for the first time, Emmett counted out the bills and rolled the coins on the same kitchen table where his brother, Johnny, cut weed.

Emmett packed the hard rolls of coins back into the coffee can when he was done, but while Emmett was at work the next day, Johnny took the can to buy more weed. When Emmett returned and found his can hollow, Johnny did not apologize, but he did offer to roll him a fresh one. It was, Emmett remembered, a nice gesture, but after that, he began keeping his can in the truck's glove box and did his counting in private.

Emmett did not need to worry about his brother helping himself for long because Johnny moved out of their trailer when he married Wendy Jo. With Dexter in jail and Lora in Florida, Johnny moved into his new family's old farmhouse. Given that there was a baby on the way, it made sense for him to go. Wendy Jo's parents had a bedroom for the two to share, so Johnny started driving truck, and Emmett took to working overtime to fill up the hours.

It wasn't that Emmett begrudged his brother money, but when he gave Johnny cash, Emmett noticed it got spent on video games and cigarettes. Emmett tried not to be a jerk, but Johnny had a wife and kids at home—a wife who came to Emmett each November saying she just didn't know what she was going to do about Christmas. Wendy Jo hemmed and hawed, making a pretense of it being a rough year for everyone all around. She would run her hand through her hair, pulling it back and wrapping it with an elastic band. She hated to ask, she said.

And every November, Emmett withdrew a few hundred dollars from his account and handed his sister-in-law an envelope, saying to make sure the kids got toys to unwrap.

"Emmett's a good man," Wendy Jo told her friend Peg Shane. "And besides, what does he have to spend his money on anyway?"

In return, Emmett was invited to the farmhouse for Christmas morning, and, each year, he warmed up his pickup, loaded his dog Lucy into the cab, and drove ten miles north to the old yellow homestead where the whole Delfino-Pratt family still lived. Twenty years after Johnny moved in as a teenage groom, he was still there in the back bedroom, and their kids now ranged from ages nineteen to six. Emmett and his dog walked up the crumbling cement steps together and pulled the door open.

Last year, the smell of bacon hit him first. Bacon and maple syrup. Wendy Jo was turning sausage links in a cast-iron spider, while her mother, Christine, bent to light a cigarette from the gas burner. Christine, dressed in her red flannel housecoat, held open the cupboard door and asked Wendy Jo if she was the inconsiderate asshole who drank the last of her coffee brandy. "You mean your fat ass in a glass?" said Paul Delfino as he walked past and kissed his wife on the neck.

Emmett watched the scene from the mudroom, he and his dog both dripping melted snow on the torn linoleum. It was a circus inside, with the kids tearing into loose wrapping paper, clutching new toys, and thanking Santa Claus over and over again as they chased each other through the living room, into the kitchen, around the table, and skidded in sock feet across the dirty floor. By this point, Christine had seen and heard enough. She hollered for the kids to smarten the hell up and start acting right.

Emmett involuntarily straightened his shoulders when Christine hollered. There were so many children. At least eight ran by in a blur into the back room, all hopped up on Christmas candy and scared of their grandmother's voice. The teenagers sat sullen on one of two couches, their attention directed at video games as the little ones ran by.

Emmett stood in the shadow of the doorway, having a difficult time placing who was connected and how. He would have preferred to be at his own kitchen table with his radio and quiet breakfast plate, but he spent every holiday with his brother's extended family. He did this mostly to hear any news of Rhetta Ballou.

Emmett would never ask out loud, but every year someone might mention heading over to Aunt Ada's house. And that mention of Ada might make someone say that Rhetta was finishing college again, or that Rhetta got a job in California, or that Rhetta just got back from somewhere like Boston, or that none of the kids but Rhetta ever had any ambition. Mentions of Rhetta were quick, and it took all of Emmett's focus and concentration to listen for them.

"Hey, Emmett," Christine waved when she felt the draft from the open door. "Merry Christmas." She removed her cigarette and handed Emmett a paper plate, telling him to load up before the little ones ate all the bacon.

Emmett remembered this as he watched Officer Monroe leave his driveway once again. He remembered the holiday scene because it was Friday, payday, and Emmett needed to get to the bank. He had opened a Christmas Club account for his brother's family, and he wanted to make the week's deposit.

When a teenage Emmett's new account at Fort Angus Savings initially reached one thousand dollars, the brand new bank teller asked him if he planned to invest. Since Emmett didn't exactly know what that meant, the new teller had him sit down across a polished wooden desk while she explained some options. Emmett listened closely. He brought home the bank brochures, and he placed them on the kitchen table beside a calculator and worked out some basic percentages.

This was how Emmett managed, over time, to accumulate his first one hundred thousand dollars. The new bank teller told Emmett about compounding and dollar cost averaging, and it made sense in his mind, so Emmett began dividing up his money. He had the teller set up long-term and short-term accounts, and after that, they talked about more complicated money management.

Each Friday Emmett walked in with his paycheck a half hour before the bank closed. As a teenager, all Emmett knew was that her nameplate said Cindy, and that she was new to Fort Angus. Even on a good day, squinting, Emmett was too young for her, but he looked forward to those Friday afternoons. She took his check, handed him an envelope of cash for the week, and Emmett drove home feeling like he'd just had the best day ever.

When they started investing, the pretty bank teller would lean forward over the wooden desk and scratch numbers in the margins with a pencil. Emmett smelled her vanilla lotion, and later, when she began to spend occasional nights with him at the trailer, he thought he was in love.

Emmett was crushed when Cindy moved downstate after only two years. It was the winters, she told Emmett, kissing his mouth, closing her car trunk, and waving good-bye. The winters were just too miserable.

Now, at 35, Emmett Pratt showed almost a full million dollars on the bottom line. He had trouble believing the figure when he saw his bank statement. Remembering his sister-in-law's anxious eyes each fall and his brother's easy raid on that old coffee can, Emmett tore up the statement each month, ripping it in half, and then half again until the numbers were obscured. He stuffed the paper pieces deep into the trash bin.

Even though Johnny drove truck on a regular schedule, and his father, Dexter, was, technically, employed, a little voice in the back of Emmett's head said to keep his money private. Each week, he cashed his paycheck, and each week, he still took ten percent off the top.

Emmett was glad for the money because with the way Officer Monroe kept questioning him about his aunt Sheila's murder, he figured he'd eventually have to hire Phil Compton to file some papers, or, if it got carried that far, be his court lawyer. He didn't know what lawyers cost, but he suspected his bank account ought to cover it.

6

RHETTA CONTEMPLATES POVERTY IN THE CAR.

Rhetta Ballou began the drive to Fort Angus thinking about a walk twenty years ago with Emmett Pratt up the garrison hill, through the old barracks, and back down again on the night of Aunt Joyce's wedding, and it startled her to remember the details so clearly.

Between the exit sign for Bowdoinham and the point where she once saw an owl fly low across the highway toward the salt marsh, her mind struggled to corral even more long-dead images. As Rhetta processed and sorted the details in thoughtful order, she had no way of knowing that her mother once made a nearly identical walk herself. She knew Ada gave birth as a teenager, but Ada never spoke about those moments, and Rhetta was shushed whenever she asked.

"You're here now, so what does it matter?" Ada always said.

Rhetta did not know that Ada Ballou left Nellie's house at age seventeen, pregnant. She did not know her mother hitched a ride across the border and worked under the table for the New Brunswick Diner until her belly got big enough for a customer to ask the cook why he was making such a beautiful young lady work so hard in her condition. Shamed, the owner sent Ada home and told her don't come back, so seven months after she'd first stuck her pretty thumb up and out of Fort Angus, Ada phoned Nellie from the old customs shack, and Nellie told her to start walking.

Ada walked three of the ten miles between the customs shack and Nellie's house on the old garrison hill before she saw her mother's black Pontiac. That three mile walk is what Ada believes started her labor. In fact, Ada could see the roofline of the Fort Angus Hospital down the hill in the distance as she walked from the border, and she focused on that particular roofline during each of the early contractions before Nellie's car pulled over on the opposite side of the road.

"If you walked this far, you could've made it all the way." Nellie assessed her daughter's condition and reached across to unlatch the door.

Ada could not read her mother's response to her enormous belly, but she slid into the front seat and pushed a small backpack on the floorboard between her knees. When Nellie offered her a cigarette, Ada accepted. "You're gonna need it," Nellie spoke with authority. "Lighter's in my purse."

Nellie dropped Ada at the front of the hospital with instructions to call if she wanted a ride afterward. Through ragged breaths, Ada stared at the big glass and metal revolving door of the new building, unsure of how to navigate. She'd read about this funny door in the newspaper, but she paced the walkway with her hands resting on her hips, not knowing what to do.

"Huh," Ada watched a woman carrying a small bouquet of flowers enter straight through the empty space, and then she watched another drag a small boy by the hand into the same empty space. Both women seemed to be pushed along into the building and swallowed up. So, standing as straight as she could, Ada inhaled and moved quickly as the glass door began to spin. It took her once around the full loop before she mustered the courage to step into the hallway. The revolving door was still on her mind when she walked up to the registration desk. In fact, Ada thought nonstop about that door as she was asked a million questions.

Ada didn't know about insurance, or family physicians, or anything other than the sudden shitdamnfucking pain that was happening right then to her lower belly and could she please fer-chrissakes get something to make it stop.

Afterward, as Ada lay in the hospital recovery ward on the scratchiest of scratchy sheets, she still wondered about that revolving door. Why in the world would a person make a door like that? Even though it was early September, she wondered how they kept the heat inside during the winter if the door was open and spinning all the time. She wondered how they kept the snow from piling in, too.

When the nurse wheeled a baby into the room, she paused when she saw Ada's head turned toward the window with her eyes fixed on nothing. The nurse moved toward Ada, leaving the baby silent in her little glass bed. Smiling, the nurse adjusted the white privacy curtain around Ada and fixed a warm washcloth in the sink. She ran it across Ada's pale face, folded the washcloth, and reached for a hairbrush.

"It's just a baby, sweets." The nurse pulled Ada's red hair back in long, smooth, comforting strokes. "Nothing to be scared of." The nurse rested the hairbrush on a side table, and then scooped up the baby and extended her arms toward Ada. "People have 'em every day."

Until this moment, Ada had not seen the baby. From the twilight of the medication, she thought she heard someone say it was a girl, but then Ada had slipped off into a long and nothingness sleep.

Now, in the light of morning, there was her daughter wiggling on her lap. On a base level, Ada had known she was pregnant, knew a baby was coming, but none of the specific details had occurred to her. Even when Nellie dropped her off in front of that crazy door, and Ada was taken to a room to undress, she still didn't figure on a real, live baby. Until then, she felt things moving in slow motion or under water or through some kind of pudding, but now with a little baby girl staring straight back at her, in the wake of the nurse's sudden kindness, Ada started to feel panic.

Slowly, the nurse explained how to wash the baby, how to feed the baby, and how to change the baby's diaper. She demonstrated how to mix up the special formula and how to file down the baby's fingernails. The baby, a willing participant in the education, remained calm while Ada tried to keep up and remember the rules.

"Does she have a name?" The nurse handed a freshly fed, clean, and dry baby to Ada, and then opened a manila envelope of colored forms. Ada shook her head, still silent, and the nurse sat down, her eyes level with Ada's.

"Now sweetie," the nurse was direct. "That baby needs a name."

The nurse threw out a string of girl names, so quick that Ada didn't have time to think. It sounded like a mush of Jennifer-amy-jessica-michelle-leslie-sally, and Ada wished she'd go slower. She wished it all would go slower. "Of course," the nurse said, "I'm from the South, so I'm always partial to Southern names."

Ada looked up.

"My mama's name was Rhetta," the nurse said, and with that, Ada told her to write it on the paper. Ada said this just before she fell back to sleep, but this time with a brand new Rhetta Ballou lying on her chest.

When Ada woke for the second time, the shift had changed, and a different nurse was on duty. Nurse Karen Angus flicked open the window shade and told Ada it was time for her to go.

Karen Angus had packed up Ada's little backpack and placed it on a chair beside the plastic bag of freebies from the hospital: sanitary pads, powdered formula, and a welcome kit with baby shoes. She laid Ada's clothing on the bed, told her to get dressed, and left a yellow paper for her to sign.

With the backpack on her shoulders and the plastic bag looped around her wrist, Ada carried baby Rhetta down the long, green hospital corridor as she worked out what to do next. Ada felt her pocket for a dime, found the pay phone in the lobby, and called Nellie for a ride. Again, Nellie told her to start walking.

"You are so lucky," Christine told her. Christine was fourteen, and Joyce, six, just stared at the baby. Nellie had gone to the store for supplies, and the remaining Ballou family watched tiny Rhetta sleep curled up in a plastic laundry basket.

Rhetta knew nothing about this piece of her mother's history because Ada did not discuss it. Had she known, Rhetta might have felt a whisper of tenderness or compassion, but she was unaware of those details. When Rhetta asked about her father, Ada stopped the conversation with "that don't matter," so as Rhetta remembered the garrison hill and Joyce's wedding and Wendy Jo and the walk with Emmett Pratt, she did not think of Ada at all. In fact, her thoughts moved to another experience entirely as she watched the pine trees blur past her car window.

She didn't care for this particular memory, in fact, she hated it, but it came fast and Rhetta raised the volume of the car stereo in an effort to drown it out. But once the memory started, it sped on its own track and there was nothing to do but wish she could reach back in time and grab her teenage self by the wrist, yanking her from that car.

◦◦◦

"Winona Peletier killed Steve Angus with a hatchet in the house next door to where my mother grew up," Rhetta told Phil Compton while they drove Mrs. Compton's new Buick post-prom to the crest of the old Fort Angus garrison. Passing the faded wooden sign and beginning the short gravel ascent, she watched Phil's profile for any sign of interest. A smile, a half turn—any motion in her direction. Rhetta knew Ada had grown up in a ramshackle clapboard house just south of the hill where Nellie built the shed that later hid Steve's body. It was originally built as a pen to house Daisy the cow, Rhetta said.

"Yeah?" Phil spoke in a lazy monotone, hands on the wheel and his pre-formed pink bow tie dangling unclipped.

Taking that as encouragement, Rhetta continued. Daisy was the bane of Ada's existence. "The bane of her existence," she spoke with fingers fluttering, trying to tell the family story right. Daisy would escape the pen and rub against the neighbor ladies' clotheslines, dropping crap in their driveways and trampling cucumbers.

"Get your goddamned cow off our property before I call the police," the neighbor ladies would holler. Rhetta said this to Phil in a mock falsetto voice. Because Aunt Christine refused and Joyce was too little, Ada was left to drag the cow—protesting and mooing, two miles up the dirt road and back into the pen.

Phil stopped the car at the edge of the deserted barracks parking lot. He turned sideways to face her, his features illuminated by the speckle of lights from the village below. "Why did your family have a cow if they lived in town?"

Deflated, Rhetta had no answer. "My grandmother built the shed that held Steve's body," she repeated. "Winona Peletier buried his body in that shed."

Winona Peletier's trial was held in Fort Angus the same week as the prom, and the whole town of Fort Angus was appalled at the details. Steve had gone missing two years prior, and while everybody thought his girlfriend was strange, nobody thought she'd killed him. That is, until her ten year-old son broke down in the school guidance office.

"Poor thing," Ada said, reading the details out loud from the *Fort Angus Republican*. "Poor, poor thing."

It turned out that Winona's son had been there when the murder happened, according to the newspaper, and that instead of being a little strange, Winona Peletier was actually one hundred percent crazy in the head. Rhetta worked at the movie theater and often saw Winona in the municipal parking lot through the plate-glass lobby doors.

She was tall enough so that, if she stood up straight, her head almost touched the door frame of the bathroom, but she walked forward bent at the waist. Winona's long blond hair was parted in the middle and tucked behind her ears to show a pair of ratty, blue feather earrings. She reminded Rhetta of the carnival workers at the Fourth of July, stoop-shouldered and greasy.

Winona sometimes bought movie tickets for herself and her son while Rhetta was working the counter. Since Steve Angus had gone to high school with Ada, and Winona knew Rhetta was Ada's daughter, she always passed along a hello as Rhetta took her money and poured the Cokes. During those times Rhetta poured her Cokes, Steve Angus had been rotting under her shed. It made Rhetta shiver, but, still, she couldn't imagine Winona taking a hatchet to Steve's body. Taking a hatchet and just chopping him up like she was butchering a moose.

"Do you suppose he was dead first?" Rhetta tried to talk to Phil that night in the car, "Or do you think she actually killed him with that ax?" Phil had already placed his arm around Rhetta's shoulders and began kissing her neck.

Rhetta tried to concentrate on kissing his neck, too, but her mind was all over the murder. "What do you suppose caused the fight?" and Phil sat back, his cheeks flushed.

"This isn't happening tonight, is it?"

Rhetta knew "this" was sex, and it wasn't that she minded, but the logistics confused her.

"How does something that big fit into something so small?" she asked Rosemary Angus once during lunch. Since Rosemary was already having sex, she was the class expert. Rosemary chewed her peanut butter sandwich thoughtfully and then her answer was enigmatic, like a junior-high sage.

"It just does."

So when Rhetta was having sex for the first time in the front bench seat of Phil Compton's mother's new Buick, her mind was filled with images of Winona Peletier. And she was still trying to figure out how a person could use a hatchet to kill someone. To chop up the body, yes, but to actually do the killing seemed one hundred times more gruesome. She had pulled off her nylon stockings, working out in her mind that if Steve was sleeping and Winona gutted his neck, it might be possible. A hatchet wasn't the same as a big saw though, and as Rhetta Ballou lost her virginity, she wondered how many times Winona would have to hack Steve's neck for him to be dead.

The same night Rhetta Ballou said yes because she was all caught up in trying to figure out exactly how Winona Peletier chopped up Steve Angus, she also learned that her family was poor.

There in the driveway, after she wasn't thinking about Winona Peletier anymore, Phil kissed her goodnight and put his class ring in her hand.

"Some of the guys thought you'd be uncomfortable going out with me because you're poor, but I want you to know that it doesn't bother me at all," Phil told her after the kiss, holding her hand.

The word rattled in Rhetta's brain.

Poor?

Phil didn't notice the shift in Rhetta because she was still holding his class ring. The porch light began to flash, and they watched Ada's silhouette pass from window to window, back to her bedroom.

The word "poor" was still rattling as Rhetta opened the passenger door. She saw, not for the first time, but for the most intense time, the deep mud ruts in the driveway. The bare porch light bulb illuminated the dried bugs and dirt on the door. The overgrown lawn and chipped paint were even more pronounced. Ada's car looked haggard and trashy, and she suddenly felt ashamed that Phil had seen it.

Images of Ada rising at 5 a.m. every day and returning home from the factory at night, bringing groceries on payday flashed in her mind.

Was that poor?

Phil backed the car carefully from the driveway, and she waved good-bye. Aunt Joyce's pink shoes were a half size too big and in her happiness at wearing fancy shoes for the first time, Rhetta hadn't cared. As she walked to the door, that half size now seemed so obvious. Did people see her scrunching up her toes to keep them on all night?

Winona Peletier, with her rotting porch and broken windows next door to Nellie's old homestead—she was poor. Rhetta'd been too busy thinking about Winona and the murder and the sex and now Phil's class ring—still warm in her hand. How long had they been poor?

Rhetta remembered Ada's face when Phil climbed up the outside stairs to the farmhouse door. She had smiled weakly and positioned Rhetta for a photo against the part of the kitchen wall where the paint was clean and the flowered wallpaper intact. Rhetta now second-guessed that weak smile. Was it shame? It hadn't occurred to her before Phil made his comment, or if it had, Rhetta remembered feeling that maybe they were a little poor but at least other people didn't notice. Now, still rattling in her brain, was the proof-positive. People noticed.

Rhetta remembered carrying Phil's silver class ring in her hand. Ada and Clint had gone to bed, and she sat in the kitchen looking at the Polaroids taken earlier. There was a skinny girl with bright red hair in too-big dress and shoes, heavily made up. Rhetta's blanket-shawl looked less like a shawl and more like a cheap baby blanket. There was no image of Ada in the photograph at all, but in that Polaroid, Rhetta saw her scrimping for a secondhand dress, taking off work early to clean the house, mustering a half-smile in an old flannel shirt while she wrestled the baby's dirty hands away from the clean, shiny, smooth fabric.

Rhetta broke up with Phil the next day, but Rosemary Angus forgot that part, so it got spread around that Phil had broken up with Rhetta, which everyone could understand. Phil's mother would've made him break up with Rhetta Ballou eventually anyway, but when Rhetta nodded toward his class ring she'd placed on the picnic table in front of the ice cream shack, Phil's face showed surprise. His lower lip dropped open, and he shuffled his feet, handing her the ice cream he'd ordered and staring over her head in the direction of his mother's car.

"Do you need a ride home?"

Back in her own vehicle, an adult Rhetta recalled thinking that had been a decent thing for him to offer, but she was also glad to remember that she had chosen to walk.

7

Peg Shane's girls hitch a ride to the quarry.

*T*he day after Sheila Hollander's funeral, Peg Shane's girls, Nevaeh and Jincy, walked the three-mile stretch of dirt road toward downtown Fort Angus. It had been a rainy week, and while the past sunny days hardened most of the mud, the road was still soft at the edges. The girls wore sandals, and the prospect of sinking ankle deep on bare feet was disgusting to contemplate. The older sister, Nevie, had twenty dollars in her shorts pocket to spend down the road at Ralph's Store. She'd lifted the cash from Peg's wallet, and if Nevie'd had the nerve to steal her mother's credit card instead, she would've made her sister walk with her all the way across town to the Wal-Mart.

"Does my hair look all right?" Nevie asked a sullen thirteen-year old Jincy in the mirror before they left. Jincy didn't care, but she wanted a soda, so pretending interest, she pulled a few strays away from Nevie's face.

"It's too hot," Jincy whined as the girls closed the screen door. In August, the Fort Angus sun was brutal, and not even half a mile out, Nevie was whining, too.

"When I get my license," she said, "I am never walking anywhere again." Jincy nodded, and then added that when she got her own license, she was going to buy a hot-pink Corvette.

"Chevys suck," Nevie responded.

On Odie's advice from jail, Peg Shane had taken Sheila Hollander's old station wagon up to Emmett's shop for a new muffler, and then she planned to register Jody-Ray for kindergarten at the Fort Angus Elementary School.

She'd told her girls to stay out of trouble, and since their cable was cut off, Nevie and Jincy sat bored at the kitchen table all morning.

"Odie took care of that bill, so we're just going to have to improvise while he's away." Peg told her girls this when she finally opened the past-due notice that had been sitting on the counter for weeks.

"You mean while he's in jail," Nevie sassed, and Peg slapped her face while Jody-Ray cried for cartoons until Jincy punched his leg. Nevie found an old Scooby Doo video tape, and Jody-Ray fell asleep on the floor, curled up under an old brown afghan.

Jincy stopped to scratch a sweaty mosquito bite on her ankle, thankful they didn't have to watch their little brother all day, and as she bent over, a truck rumbled past, honking its horn and kicking up dust from the middle of the road.

"Oh, God," Nevie grabbed Jincy's arm and pulled into her sister's sweaty side. She recognized the driver as a Delfino, but could not determine which one. At least three Delfinos and a couple more Pratts worked at the feed store unloading bags of fertilizer and selling farm equipment, all sharing the same family truck. They had each worked at the feed store through high school and saw no reason to stop after graduation. Nevie did some quick math and guessed the driver to be twenty or twenty-one.

"They're, like, the hottest guys in town." This, from Nevie while Jincy shrugged, scratching another mosquito bite on her arm and trying to ignore the pink blister on her right heel. The truck stopped, and when Nevie saw the white back-up lights, she straightened her posture and grabbed Jincy's hand.

"You ladies need a ride?" a young man leaned over to roll down the passenger-side window.

Even though Nevie was not a hundred percent sure of his identity, she'd narrowed him down to a few good possibilities, so she opened the door and climbed up without hesitation, dragging a reluctant Jincy behind her. The interior of the truck reeked of pine-tree air freshener and cologne. There were no seatbelts, and the floorboards were caked with sawdust and fertilizer.

"Nice floor lights," Nevie pointed to the red additions circling the base of the interior.

"Whore lights," he answered, and Nevie laughed at the rhyme.

The young man turned up the radio dial, and the heavy bass distortion made the girls' ears go numb. They could feel the vibration through the seats, and it seemed as if the entire truck cab was shaking. "So, what about that murder?" he hollered over the heady sounds. He meant the murder of Sheila Hollander, as it was all anyone in Fort Angus was talking about. With one hand on the steering wheel, he turned his head to watch Nevie and Jincy's face for a response. "You're the Shane girls, right?"

Nevie shrugged, and Jincy watched the potato fields move past, their blossoms high and ripe, as she caught a bit of a breeze from the truck's open window. Neither girl spoke because there was nothing to say. As the mother of their mother's boyfriend, Sheila Hollander had been a grandmother to all of them, even though Jody-Ray was her own blood and, technically, the only kid she needed to favor.

Sheila wasn't like others, who made a pretense of saying over and over again how the girls were "just like family." Sheila treated them like family, loading them into the old station wagon and buying them all the same ice creams. Sheila carted them to McDonald's for hamburgers and to the Wal-Mart for new shoes.

Sheila once gave the girls an old box of jewelry craft supplies to share, with bits of lace and glitter and little tubes of sequins. Both girls spent an entire afternoon gluing beads onto cut-up pieces of cardboard.

"Beautiful," Sheila had said when she hung the glittery pictures, still tacky from too much white glue, on her fridge with dusty magnets.

And now, bouncing over potholes in a beat-up pickup, Nevie didn't want to talk details. She did not want to describe how Sheila Hollander, the closest thing she had to an actual grandmother, had been stabbed with a knife in the neck so hard it almost cut her head all the way off, so she bent forward to tighten her sandal buckle instead. Bending forward shifted her halter top above her waistband, exposing the fake butterfly tattoo she'd made Jincy place on her lower back that morning. The driver noticed, and he moved his hand from the steering wheel to trace the blue and silver design.

"Cool," he said, and his thumb gave Nevie a line of tiny goosebumps. She took an extra moment to straighten up, and in that extra moment, Jincy turned from the truck's window and stared over her sister's back.

"Did you know that Nevie's full name is Heaven spelled backwards?"

The driver did not, but he said that was cool, too.

"Jincy is short for Jincelle. Mum made up that name special," she continued. "I'm thirteen last week."

He moved his hand from Nevie's back, until Nevie spoke up. "I'm almost eighteen," she lied. The driver, by this time Nevie had him pegged for Troy, Ross, or Junior, relaxed his neck muscles a bit, and then he mentioned the murder again. He heard that someone cut her head clean off, and that it was found in the bathroom with little pieces of the rest of her in corners throughout the trailer. He heard that whoever done it was a devil worshipper and made a 666 with her blood on the front door. And, he heard the police were hunting down a terrorist connection, too. He said it wouldn't surprise him, seeing as how Fort Angus was right on the border.

He told the girls all that he'd heard, until Jincy threatened to get out of the truck and walk home. So Nevie took charge and said she couldn't think of anything more fun than driving up to the quarry pools to swim. She said it in a way that made him think it was his idea though, so when he extended his arm across the back of the bench seat, Nevie snuggled closer.

They stopped at Ralph's for supplies. Ralph's was a unique combination of gas station, sandwich shop, and liquor store. On any given day, a half dozen old men in flannel shirts leaned over Ralph's porch railing with Styrofoam cups of black coffee, their trucks parked in a line. The liar's club, they called themselves. These men would talk for hours.

Inside, Ralph's offered shelves of dusty cracker boxes and antacid at three times the cost of Wal-Mart or Rite Aid. Pizza specials were written in cursive with a fat red marker on a paper plate and thumb-tacked to the wall.

Nevie and Jincy stayed in the idling truck, while their driver hefted two six packs, one orange soda and the other Budweiser, into the cab. Twenty-one, thought Nevie, narrowing the driver's identity even more.

He nodded in the direction of the liar's club, who looked from the girls to the young man and back again with disapproval. Disapproval, except for Dexter Pratt, who winked and grinned.

"Don't you have to work?" Jincy asked, sipping her soda from the corner of the truck cab. He laughed and said he was on an extended lunch break.

Six miles down an old dirt access road was the trail to the

quarry pit. Half a dozen cars lined up along the access road already, and the girls recognized a few of the vehicles. The black truck was their Uncle Sam's.

They picked their way along the trail, single file, following the thud of country music until they heard voices just beyond the pine trees.

"I dare you," a woman coaxed, and a splash of water echoed. When they cleared the trees, the quarry was before them in a mean and clean cut of granite. Steep ledges jutted on either side of the quarry pool, and two young men in cutoff jeans stood on its highest point.

"If Sam can do it, what's your problem?" The woman's voice, framed by an orange bikini on a dirty blue towel, was Wendy Jo's. Wendy Jo was much older than Nevie, was, in fact, best friends with her mother, but Nevie waved anyway. The two young men on the ledge saw the girls, and shamed by the new audience, both took two running steps and leaped.

For a moment, the jumpers seemed caught in a slow-motion freeze frame, and Nevie and Jincy watched them hang suspended with wide eyes. And then, an instant later, they were in the water. "Holy shit," they sputtered when they surfaced, swimming to the shoreline where they emerged with cutoff jeans sticking heavy to their white legs.

"Hey," Wendy Jo said, "nice jail bait."

The rest of the crowd turned toward Nevie and Jincy and laughed. But it was a good-natured, joke-sharing laugh, and Nevie didn't feel like she was being made fun of.

When Wendy Jo reminded the crowd that these were Sam's nieces, loosely connected to the Sheila Hollander murder, the crowd drew in for details. Wendy Jo offered Nevie her joint and motioned for her to share a piece of the towel.

Again, Nevie thought, again with the details.

Just when Wendy Jo asked if Sheila Hollander was really decapitated like they heard, Sam Shane emerged from the quarry trail.

"What the hell?" Sam stood hunched and pale in his shorts, soaking wet from his last jump, and goose-fleshed from the walk down the path. Nevie recognized the marijuana smell on her uncle, too, but she smiled, saying "hey Uncle Sam," and Sam, for his part, grabbed Nevie's wrists and pulled them wide, exposing the short halter top.

"Damn, girl," he spoke. "You've grown."

With her uncle's endorsement, Nevie sat on the side of the quarry bank, pulling Jincy down with her. The next hour had Nevie accepting a warm can of beer while Jincy scowled at the gum wrappers and potato chip bags scattered on the ground by the crowd.

Talk turned to Miles Compton, home from downstate or somewhere. "He gives me the creeps," said Wendy Jo, emphasizing "creeps" as if it was a word with two distinct syllables. Nevie was grateful for something to discuss other than the back and forth of Sheila's grisly details, and she nodded in agreement, even though she'd never met Miles Compton before.

"Fucking homo came into the shop today," said Sam, and he

he spat the word, as if there was nothing more vile to contemplate than "homo." His jaw was tight, and his mouth turned up into a thin, little sneer. He crushed his empty beer can and threw it toward the water, pretending not to notice when it fell short and rolled down a small embankment, landing near a rotten tree stump.

Miles Compton's visit pissed Sam off enough to spit in front of the crowd. "Fucking Emmett Pratt, too," he said, snatching another can from the cooler.

Nevie did her best to gather details from context as the group nodded. She heard her uncle mutter that it was just what this hole of a town needed, more queers and queer-lovers, and she put together that Emmett Pratt had made Sam work on the Compton family Buick that morning, and now Sam was worried he might have AIDS, given that Miles Compton ass-fucked a minor last year.

"Or," Sam Shane said, "maybe that minor ass-fucked him." Either way, Sam continued, he'd bust the face of any man who tried to put a hand near his own ass.

Nevie knew enough to shut up, even though she wanted to ask for clarification, given that she didn't think you could get AIDS from just standing near a person. Nevie watched her uncle pull Wendy Jo Pratt into the woods, but Wendy Jo ran back out, grabbed her blue towel, and winked at Nevie before stepping back into the thick of the pine trees.

Their driver had taken his shirt off, and Nevie tried unsuccessfully not to stare. He was slim and cut, and he stretched out right beside her, resting on his elbows. No fat on him, Nevie thought, watching his chest move up and down with each breath. He had, like every man in Aroostook County, a farmer's tan that ended in pale white at the marker of his short-sleeved T-shirt. She was especially interested in the soft, light brown hair on the young man's belly. The line of hair stopped short at his waistband, and she resisted the urge to reach for it.

Nevie also resisted the urge to ask about the black tattoo wrapped around his forearm, but she wondered about its design. "Tribal," he said, when he caught her staring.

"What tribe?" she asked, and he laughed.

Then he called her naïve. She didn't know what was so naïve about asking what tribe, but she wanted to stay there in the shade of the hot sun, so she laughed too.

"So," the young man leaned in to her ear. "How old are you really?"

Nevie wondered how old she needed to be, as she brought her hand up to touch his pale neck.

8

MILES COMPTON TAKES HIS MOTHER'S CAR TO BE SERVICED WHILE HIS FATHER CHANNELS MR. EXCEPTIONAL.

*O*n the same August day that Peg Shane's girls hitched a ride to the quarry pit, and well before Rhetta Ballou received the call that Wendy Jo was in crisis, prompting her early-morning drive home to Fort Angus, Miles Compton had no idea that he'd later play a role in solving Sheila Hollander's murder. All he knew was that his mother's car needed an oil change, and that after today his father would be living in the Fort Angus facility for the elderly.

"Sonuva whore," Miles heard the rattle of a tool against metal and then the sound of glass shattering on concrete. He heard another expletive, louder.

"Sonuva jeezily friggin' whore," with emphasis on the "jeezily," followed by the thud of something falling again. He had hesitated before leaving his mother's old Buick in the parking lot, and he looked in the direction of the machine shop as he walked.

The shop was a large, square annex to the Irving station. It held two bays with lifts and grease pits beneath. Miles had taken his mother's car for service, and he stood awkwardly in the corner of the building, shifting from one foot to the other and concentrating on the outdated nudie calendars that lined the little waiting area to the left of the garage bay. The waiting area had two vinyl chairs, both ripped with stained foam stuffing spilling onto the floor, but Miles chose to stand as he watched the old car hoisted up.

The man, a Shane, Miles suspected because of his freckles and short stature, was angry. He didn't say as much, but Miles watched the man's body language as Emmett Pratt stood at the door with his hands crossed behind his back.

Miles suspected the Shane had been about to say no, that the empty garage was booked solid with jobs for the day, and he expected to be filled up every time Miles brought his fag pervert self around. Miles suspected that had the Shane been allowed to speak, he would have offered to beat his sorry, fucked-up, homo ass.

As it happened, Emmett Pratt was on the schedule that day, and he watched Miles drive up to the oil bay. He recognized the old Buick as Lyddy Compton's, and he'd heard about the trouble Miles had gotten himself into. Both the gay part and the seventeen-year-old boyfriend part. He'd heard about it from the shop guys, but Emmett was, himself, in the middle of a public opinion storm. Emmett also calculated the age difference between his own teenaged self and his first bank-teller love, then the age difference between the shop rats and their girlfriends, and with all that in his mind, he figured that, not knowing one hundred percent of the facts, there was no reason to turn away good business.

So, when Emmett saw Miles enter the waiting room, he walked the short distance around the bay and into the annex, positioning his body directly in Sam Shane's sight line. He did this to ensure customer service, and Emmett stood by for the entire oil change while Miles continued to watch Sam Shane's face.

Sam Shane's mouth had tightened into a sour line, and he looked from Emmett to Miles without comment as he slammed each tool against the car's undercarriage.

When the oil change was finished, Sam wiped his hands with a rag and tossed the keys to Emmett. "You write up the ticket," he'd said, glaring at Miles. "I'm done." Sam Shane turned, walked toward his own truck, and then spun out the gravel parking lot.

For his part, Miles handed Emmett cash, folded the receipt into his pocket, and drove home to help pack his father's belongings.

It wasn't so bad that Lyddy left him, but she left him for Dexter Pratt, and that's why Mayor Joel Compton still felt the rage all these years later. With no idea that Emmett, or any Pratt, would ever own anything more than a rusty spot in the trailer park and an old pickup truck, it was easy to believe the entire Pratt family was trash.

The mayor sat in his kitchen chair with the newspaper unfolded across the table. The photo showed Emmett on the courthouse steps, but the mayor saw only the shadow of Dexter's features in the blurry black-and-white image.

Dexter Pratt did road construction during the hot summer months, and when the state laid off each November, Dexter collected unemployment until the April rehire. Even though Mayor Compton made sure Dexter Pratt went to jail for kidnapping Lyddy, as well as for auto theft, he had also seen the yellow suitcase packed neatly in the trunk of Lyddy's new car. In fact, he continued seeing the image of his wife's suitcase in his mind for decades afterward. That scene ran full-paced alongside the memories of Dexter Pratt loitering in the municipal parking lot, Dexter Pratt spitting Skoal into an old plastic Mountain Dew bottle, and Dexter Pratt winking boldly at Lyddy, even on the night of his arrest.

Dexter Pratt was trash, and Joel Compton was the mayor of Fort Angus. The mayor had given Lyddy a brand-new Buick for her birthday the summer she'd run off. Phil was starting for the varsity basketball team that year, and it was also the year Lyddy got pregnant with Miles. Mayor Compton was thrilled with his new son, and the photos from back then showed a beaming Joel Compton holding brand new Miles up for all the town council to see. The mayor, oblivious to any speculation, hoped baby Miles might settle his wife down in her middle age.

"Lots of women," he told an embarrassed, teenaged Phil, "lots of women have babies in their mid-thirties."

Active in the Rotary, Mayor Compton had just been elected for the first time that year, and he had accepted with a blushing and thankful speech that ran twenty minutes over the council's official agenda. It was a good speech, he remembered, as he'd been able to invoke both God and the pro-life agenda. He thought of the men on the council who had slapped his back in congratulations that night.

As a result of the election, he appeared almost weekly in the *Fort Angus Republican*, holding oversized scissors to cut ribbons or handing trophies to winning teams.

As a lawyer, Mayor Compton worked so that Lyddy could stay home, but even with a new baby that year, Lyddy tended to rattle around their house, a raised ranch situated in a line of other raised ranches across the newer section of Fort Angus. She rattled around the house, cleaning obscure corners, wiping appliances, and making dozens of tiny, hard oatmeal cookies each week for the church social hour.

These memories played out in Mayor Compton's mind on the day of his diagnosis. From the chair opposite the doctor's desk with Lyddy by his side, he had listened to Doctor Benis, but he wasn't having any of it. He was too young, too fit for this dementia, and hell if he was going to end up rotting at some state-run nursing home. He said as much to Lyddy on the drive back to the house. The mayor gripped Lyddy's knee tightly as she steered the Buick, making her promise on her life not to put him in a nursing home.

No, no. When Mayor Compton shared that his mind played some strange tricks, transporting him back to that one terrible summer every time he drank his coffee, for instance, he was hoping Dr. Benis would advise taking Lyddy downstate to Old

Orchard Beach for some vacation time. They could rent a motel room across the street from the pier, eat the free doughnuts for breakfast in the lobby, and then walk the length of the public beach together. At night, the mayor figured they could explore the vendor stalls lining each side of the pier. He doubted Lyddy would get her palm read or her hair braided, but she might like a shirt with their names painted across the front.

Stress, that's what he was hoping Dr. Benis would say.

When Dr. Benis said early-onset, unexplained, and rapidly advancing dementia at age 65, Mayor Compton wished Lyddy had not driven him to the appointment that day, and he wished she was not sitting right beside him to hear the doctor's words.

He'd just won the Fourth of July Mr. Exceptional Contest for the seventh year in a row, and even though Dr. Benis was outlining options and new drugs, all Mayor Compton could imagine was some other man winning the town's womanless beauty pageant next summer. Any other man would treat it like a joke, and that fact, much more than losing his mind to dementia, was too much for Mayor Compton's brain to contemplate.

Had he known the most recent pageant would be his last, he would have splurged for the expensive makeup he'd seen advertised on the late-night cable channel, and he would have sent away for bigger falsies at the official breast cancer website.

Instead, he dragged out last year's plastic tackle box from the corner recesses of the garage. He stored two tackle boxes in the garage corner. The metal tackle box held his long abandoned fishing flies, and the plastic tackle box contained his collection of cosmetics.

Every small town celebrates Independence Day, but none as doggedly as Fort Angus, Maine. With winters lasting six months and temperatures that freefall well below zero, Aroostook County people earn their holiday.

Imagine the heroic amount of determination to rise winter morning after winter morning, step down barefoot onto a shockingly cold floor, walk through a frigid house and its mudroom, slip on wool socks and tall boots, throw a parka over pajamas, move outside to a car, praying the locks haven't frozen, and then listening to the engine's high-pitched shriek as it tries to turn over. It takes a resilient soul to burrow toes deep into socks and a body even deeper into a jacket, exhaling through a scarf and watching breath condense and then freeze on the wool as the engine squeals, stalls, and then starts again—this time with a lower whine of resignation. On any February morning in Fort Angus, driveways are lined with reams and billows of white car exhaust, as the owners have run back inside for a shower and breakfast during the twenty minutes it takes to warm up a vehicle.

From no other perspective could a person actually look forward to mud season, but mud season is welcomed in late April and all through May, when the last of the spring blizzards are finished and the sun begins to melt away the several feet of packed snow.

The grocery store orders extra wooden pallets for people with soft driveways, and the pallets are laid end to end in a trail from driveway to doorstep, as they form ruts into spongy lawns. Throughout Fort Angus, men hose off dried mud from work boots and dismayed mothers pluck stumbling children up by the shoulders, hollering at them for ruining good sneakers.

As mud season wears on, Fort Angus sheds its layers. The men at the feed store unload their pallets in short-sleeves instead of flannel. Lyddy Compton walks down the aisle of the Imperial Baptist Sanctuary in white sandals, and Karen Angus brings her cuttings to the community plant sale to watch people move up the garden line and marvel at her bright-pink tulips, the bulbs forced up through potting soil with lights in her basement.

Slowly, as if not quite believing winter is over, that there might still be one big one left, Fort Angus crawls toward the sun. The dairy bar opens up at the end of May, and Rosemary Angus, now Rosemary Compton, serves out strawberry frappés and brownies á la mode with her perky friends. Slowly, Fort Angus changes its seasons, and when June finally arrives with its sun, it is time for eager and triumphant Independence Day plans.

Each year, the fair committee booked Circus Frank to do acrobatic tricks for the kids. There was the Alligator Man, a pig scramble, demolition derby, lawn-mower races, tractor pulls, a country gospel band up from South Carolina for the lawn-chair concert, and a blinking midway with rickety thrill rides and water-pistol games.

Young couples hold hands and stroll the length of the community park as the carnival workers try to steal their attention with a string of "hey, pretty girl" and offers to throw in a second ring toss absolutely free. The smell of fried dough with cinnamon sugar mixes with the smell of hot dogs and onions, and those warm scents override the tang of the portable toilets and the exhaust fumes from the demolition derby.

Apart from the parade, the fireworks, and the midway rides, the crowd looked most forward to the Mr. Exceptional Contest. Each year, Fort Angus men of prominence compete in a mock beauty pageant, and the winner is crowned Mr. Exceptional.

Just before his son Miles came home and just before he would be deemed a risk and committed to the long-term-care assisted-living facility, Mayor Joel Compton drew his heavy body across the temporary stage in a silver evening gown. The other men in the competition, friends from the Rotary or colleagues down at the Chamber of Commerce, had quickly stuffed balloons or volleyballs against their hairy chests and pulled whatever would fit over their bulky bodies from their wives' closets. There were caftans and turbans, and plenty of granny-style panties. The men vamped and sang, limp-wristed, with affected soprano voices.

Mayor Compton, though, had ordered special contoured falsies from a breast-cancer website and the two-sided tape to secure them. He bought a long blond wig and spent two full Saturdays brushing and spraying it into an elaborate braided style.

The new guy at the shoe store scratched his head the first time Mayor Compton turned up with seamed stockings, wanting to try on any ladies high heel that might fit his big feet, but he figured it was all in good fun. He brought out box after box as the mayor stretched his leg in front of the mirror, finally settling on a pair of red patent leather pumps.

"Mayor Compton sure does have the community spirit," the new guy told his wife that night over supper, and when Mayor Compton glided smoothly across the stage with the satin Mr. Exceptional sash once again, the whole town applauded from their lawn chairs. Mayor Compton saw camera flashes as he waved and blew kisses.

While the other men changed from their costumes, Mayor Compton remained in his gown and walked the length of the midway among the couples and the small children pulling on the arms of their parents, begging for just one more carousel ticket. Mayor Compton strolled past the men gearing up for the truck pulls, past the agricultural displays, blue-ribboned animals, and the lawnmower races already in progress. Mayor Compton walked the length of the midway carnival and back again, moving slowly and spinning, showing off his winning sash to the applause of the carnival workers.

"Yup," Mayor Compton overheard the new guy at the shoe store tell his wife again after the pageant as they settled into lawn chairs for the country gospel music concert. "Our mayor sure does have some community spirit."

And now? Now Lyddy wanted to take that all away from him. She wanted to stick him in some state-run dementia ward, and he was not having it. He called Phil for help. In fact, he called all his friends and business colleagues. He dug out his worn leather address book and went down the list, number by number.

He explained the situation as a matter of grave, grave importance, and it actually made Lyddy's decision very easy when she came home from the grocery store and found her husband holding the telephone. He looked triumphant and smug, meeting her eyes directly as he spoke into the receiver.

"Hello? Yes, this is Mr. Exceptional calling, and I need a favor."

9

RHETTA CONSIDERS VIOLENCE AND THE RELIABILITY OF HER MEMORIES.

One hour into the drive, and Rhetta stopped in Augusta for a snack at the Barnes & Noble Starbucks counter. Instead of coffee, she bought hot fruit-flavored tea, and chose a slice of lemon loaf, too. As she paid the green-aproned cashier five dollars, she wondered what her mother would say about such an expensive treat. Five dollars, and all she got was a cup of tea and a pastry. Rhetta heard Ada say for that price she could have bought a whole box of tea bags and a whole package of cookies. She heard Ada's voice tell her she was a damned fool with her money.

As she walked across the parking lot, Rhetta saw the changing colors of the first fall leaves. Aroostook County moved four weeks ahead of the state for leaf season, and as Rhetta traveled farther north, she watched the colors show brighter with each mile. What started as a quick splash of red when she entered the highway in Portland were now large areas of orange and yellow in Augusta.

As she placed the paper cup carefully in the drink holder and waited for her tea to cool, Rhetta broke off a corner of the lemon loaf and her thoughts returned to Emmett Pratt.

When Emmett Pratt was first questioned for the murder of Sheila Hollander, Ada called to tell Rhetta, but she didn't believe it. Neither did Ada. Even though Rhetta had not regularly seen Emmett Pratt in two decades, she knew Emmett was no killer.

First, there was no motive. No motive at all. Second, Emmett once walked the full length of Fort Angus and back, three times over in the dark, right beside Rhetta, carrying her shoes, and she never felt the tiniest bit unsafe. In fact, during the whole mess of that crazy year, when the world was crumbling straight through Rhetta's fingers, walking silent with Emmett Pratt on the night Aunt Joyce got married was the one, single spot of ease she could remember.

For her mother, it came down to a visceral disbelief that a boy who pumped gas into her car, washed her windows, and checked her oil level was capable of such violent action. Ada was a decent judge of character, and her bones told her that Emmett Pratt was getting screwed.

"Has Hartley actually arrested him?" Rhetta asked her mother on the telephone, aware that the act of an arrest made no difference at all in the court of Fort Angus opinion. Ada told her that Hartley Monroe wouldn't recognize his ass from a toilet pipe, and Rhetta wasn't sure if that meant yes or no.

◦∾◦

Rhetta remembered Hartley Monroe as a brand-new officer when it was just her and Ada in a rented house on Bluebell Road. The house was small, gray, and boxlike, with a backyard big enough to plant a vegetable garden, and that garden was the reason Hartley Monroe showed up at the door.

Hartley Monroe believed Ada's tomato plants were a front for growing marijuana, and he parked in the field across the road, watching from the front seat of his cruiser. He'd eventually stride up the driveway and ask to look around, scanning the perimeter and poking Ada's side garden plot with an old stick he found in the ditch.

"Hartley Monroe is an asshole," Ada had said, staring at him through the curtain, and a very young Rhetta nodded from habit. Lamen Hollander had just shot himself, and Ada thought most people in town were assholes. Rhetta watched her flip off Hartley Monroe from the kitchen window as he drove away.

This is the image Rhetta had in her head when Ada called to tell her about the murder: Hartley Monroe poking around Emmett's trailer with a stick, which, all things considered, was not that far off from Emmett's actual experience.

Rhetta felt connected to Emmett, not just because of the walk they shared on that summer night, but because for a while, his aunt Sheila Hollander was something like a grandmother to her.

Sheila had two sons, far apart in age. When Ada took up with the oldest, Lamen Hollander, she was very much in love. A bear of a man with big hands and a huge, beard-covered smile, Lamen was back from Vietnam and told stories of scraping flesh and human remains from the leaves covering the roof of his shelter—stories that made Rhetta's mouth hang open and a Popsicle melt in her hand. It was like Jell-O, he said—laughing, and she imagined what it must be like to shovel Jell-O off a roof in the jungle.

"What's heroin?" Rhetta asked when she overheard them talking on the porch one night after supper. The two sat with their shoulders touching, Ada's face looking up at Lamen's as she placed her empty coffee mug on the bottom step. The summer skyline had just begun to turn orange in the twilight and Rhetta was about to beg for change to get some penny candy, but Lamen's mouth tensed, and Ada's smile dropped. Ada handed her a whole dollar from her denim skirt pocket, and without even telling her to wash her face, shooed her out down the road toward Nellie's house.

A craftsman and a carpenter by trade, Lamen Hollander spent his days hitched over the walls of unfinished houses and straddling saw horses. His power tools had thick orange cords that Rhetta was told to stay away from when Ada brought his thermos each afternoon.

Lamen once carved Rhetta's name into a piece of pine board. He painted the carved portion pink and silver, and then he varnished the whole board to shining. Rhetta hugged the board tight in her arms like a baby, and thanked Lamen over and over again. In fact, Rhetta jumped onto Lamen's back for a hug, and he piggybacked her to where Ada sat at the kitchen table having a cigarette with Sheila Hollander. Sheila's youngest boy, Odie, a surprise, was sprawled under the table, drawing pictures of cars on the back of cut-up breakfast cereal boxes.

Ada told Sheila how impressed she was with Lamen's wood-working, and Sheila beamed while Ada hung the carved board onto Rhetta's bedroom wall.

Later that afternoon, when Lamen Hollander pulled the old car to the side of a dirt road behind Nellie's house and began to beat on Ada, it was a surprise. Rhetta was coloring in the back-seat, bent unaware over a tablet of construction paper when the car bumped her crayons with a start, forcing the box to the floor. When she looked up, Ada reached for the door, and Rhetta saw Lamen grip a whole handful of hair, jerking Ada's head back toward the steering wheel.

"Run," Ada shrieked, wrestling with Lamen Hollander in the front seat and kicking the door open with her feet.

On instinct, Rhetta obeyed. She ran fast, but when she climbed up the garrison hill to Nellie's house, panting and scratched from bursting down the shortcut path and through the overgrown raspberry bushes, Nellie sat unaffected at her kitchen table. She put down her cigarette and told Christine to get the Kool Aid from the refrigerator.

"Oh, it can't be that bad," she said opaquely in response to Rhetta's sweaty panic.

Proving the point, Christine took Rhetta's hand with her

cigarette-free one, and together they walked to the end of the dooryard, peering down the hill to see if the car was still there at the end of the road.

It was not.

"See?" Christine pointed. "It wasn't that bad."

Rhetta was still crying on the porch with her Kool-Aid cup when Ada's car pulled in ten minutes later. Lamen and Ada got out in slow motion, and Rhetta watched keenly for any reaction. Her mother carried a paper sack of cucumbers from her garden and walked straight toward the house with Lamen following behind. There was no quickened pace, no secret "help me" glance, and at that moment Rhetta considered that maybe she had imagined the beating. Through the window, she watched her mother sit down at the table, divvying cucumbers and asking Lamen to find her a lighter.

She wondered if she had dreamed that scene in the car with Ada's head twisted back, her bright-red hair tangled around Lamen's clenched fist, but then she thought no. The details were too fresh and too vivid, and the sound of her mother's voice was too clear, telling her to run, to run now.

Even as an adult, far removed from the threat of physical violence, Rhetta sorted through specifics of that day on her grandmother Nellie's front porch and felt doubt. As she cataloged the images in her mind, she struggled for any proof that her memory was real. She questioned herself and the faded edges of the details. Why would Lamen Hollander have hit Ada? Why wouldn't Nellie have reacted? Why would Ada stay with Lamen?

With time and perspective, it made no rational sense to Rhetta, but the scenes still existed in her mind.

As she drove, dredging up more and more long-locked images, another scene played out, and this one felt like proof, validation that she had, in fact, seen what she'd seen and there was no way her mind would construct such random acts on its own.

Later that same summer a young Rhetta was roused from her bed by a commotion. Her room was dark, and she remembered feeling her way alongside the wall and into the tiny hallway. She saw her mother illuminated from the stark bulb above the kitchen sink.

"What, are you going to shoot me?" Ada mocked, standing directly in front of Lamen as he walked into the mudroom. It was late, and she had just turned out the porch light when Lamen arrived at the house on Bluebell Road, gun in hand. The truck was shut off in the driveway, and Rhetta heard a distinct series of popcorn pops from outside the window. This, she thought later, is what woke her up.

"Go ahead," Ada challenged, up in his face with her back arched and her finger pointed. "Go ahead and shoot me."

Lamen slid his body against the mudroom wall, his elbow catching on the wooden chair board. Lamen had not expected Ada to speak, let alone hold out her arms wide. The rifle barrel dipped for a moment and then rested against Ada's chest where her red hair struggled out of its metal barrette. Rhetta watched Lamen's red eyes close just before he dropped down to his knees.

Ada followed Lamen's sightline, realized Rhetta's presence, and waved behind herself, "Go get under your bed." Sensing Rhetta's hesitation, she hollered, "Now!"

Rhetta scooted down the hallway and slid between the box spring and the carpet. The cardboard crates of spare clothing and Christmas ornaments were still pushed aside from the last time she'd been there. Moving them exposed a spot where the kittens had pooped, and the poops had shriveled into hard little rocks. She watched the poops as she laid on her stomach, listening toward the kitchen, and wondered about those new kittens and if they were really shot dead like Lamen had just said. She wondered what she'd do if Lamen did shoot Ada, who she'd live with and where she'd go if she did not have her mother. Aunt Christine, probably. Or maybe Aunt Joyce.

She rested an ear against the floor and tried to hear better, but she just heard muffled voices and then nothing. She woke up the next morning in her own bed, and no mention was made as her mother made toast and coffee for Lamen.

After breakfast, they asked if she wanted to drive out to the quarry when the rain cleared up, and she wondered if maybe she dreamed the last night's events. Lamen brought home a new gray kitten, and Rhetta eventually forgot about the two that disappeared.

Back in the car as an adult, Rhetta processed this second moment of fear and violence with a sense of distance and distracted disbelief in the same way she remembered being at Nellie's house on the day she watched Ada get knocked in the head, and then ten minutes later sit safely at the kitchen table divvying up cucumbers.

Rhetta's tea had cooled enough to sip carefully, and she focused on its bitter taste. The one time she had mentioned Lamen to her mother as an adult, Ada's voice had lowered. It was not an apology, but undertones of regret were contained in her direct and simple statement.

"That war ruined him, Rhetta. You don't understand."

Rhetta nodded and Ada changed the subject. Rhetta supposed it was true, and she could not understand. She also supposed a war would ruin a person.

As Rhetta drove, images of Lamen Hollander likening his tour in Vietnam to scraping Jell-O off jungle leaves played in her head, and she suspected that a person just couldn't return to Fort Angus any kind of normal after an experience like that.

But, considering the hard physical violence directed toward her mother, Rhetta also wondered how such a strong and proud Ballou woman would put herself in the middle of that relationship. Not just put herself in the middle, but stay. Stay, and believe she was happy. Rhetta wanted to ask her mother what she was thinking when she chose Lamen Hollander to be part of their lives.

Rhetta had little doubt that if Lamen Hollander's body had not been found slumped over his steering wheel, a bullet hole in his head from his own gun, that Ada would still be with him.

And, as soon as Rhetta got into the judgmental part of her mind, wondering how Ada could have let a man hit her, she remembered one particular year with one particular man of her own. Instead of sticking around to take a physical hit, Rhetta had turned tail and run.

This particular man, a teacher, forced her out of her own hometown nearly twenty years ago. Images of his eyes, gray as the water of the cold Abnaki River, filled her mind. She remembered the feel of his arms folding around her young limbs and the sensation of heat from his body. Rhetta remembered that when circled by this man's strength, she could relax. As she pressed her face into his chest and let him stroke the length of her hair, she felt safe. She felt protected, and she imagined that this feeling was not so different from how Lamen made Ada feel. That by crawling into the warm nook-space of Lamen Hollander's arms, Ada could let go for a moment and believe that she was not in this hard life alone.

Yes, when Rhetta thought about those memories, she could not blame Ada for putting them both in the path of Lamen's uncertain violence. She suspected that for her mother, the trade-off was worth it. That Ada would take a hit or two in exchange for feeling safe beside Lamen. Or, that Lamen would change. Or, that with time, Ada could coax those poison war memories out of his head with the promise of a thermos in the afternoons and hot breakfast in the mornings.

She understood her mother's perspective because she had believed the same things from her teacher man. That he would leave his pregnant wife. That he would pluck her from the prospect of going directly from high school graduation to the glove-factory line. That he loved her. That she was not in this hard life alone.

Rhetta pushed the teacher man from her head as she drank from the paper cup in big gulps, not caring that her lips were being scalded. The pain from the hot water helped sharpen her thinking. Her mind was wandering into a space she wasn't ready to explore, and the burn in her mouth brought her head back in line.

Specifics, that was what she was grasping for. Specific details to reinforce that as a little girl, she had, indeed, been privy to very violent scenes. Resolved to focus her thinking, Rhetta Ballou again noted details of the day she walked the length of Nellie's packed dirt dooryard.

She had circled Ada's car as it sat parked in a mud puddle closest to the road. She studied her reflection in the dusty car window. Sweaty ponytail, sticky T-shirt, thick glasses, purple smile. She had made a face at the reflection. And then another. The reflection looked back with crossed eyes and a lolling tongue.

Rhetta smooshed her nose hard against the window, fogging up the space with her breath. Wiping the steam from the glass, she saw her crayons scattered on the floor of the back seat, and then, suddenly, there was the part she'd been hoping to retain. There, among her crayons in a jumble, lay a big clump of her mother's red hair on the floorboard.

10

LYDDY COMPTON FINDS RELIGION.

*T*here were many reasons Lyddy Compton enjoyed the Sunday services at Fort Angus Imperial Baptist Sanctuary. The church itself was pretty, a tall brick building with brightly colored stained-glass renderings of Bible scenes. Her favorite panel was the interpretation of Adam and Eve before the tree of life. Eve's blonde hair hung long and sensuous, and Adam's white body was hidden behind intricately wrought pieces of green glass representing shrubbery and fig leaves.

There was a debate about whether or not to transfer the old windows to the new church upon its completion, and Lyddy had been torn. On the one hand, she understood the new reverend's point. The windows would be expensive to move, and God required no artistic ornamentation, especially ornamentation that featured naked women.

But on the other hand, and, well, now that Lyddy thought about it, there really was no other hand. She remembered being torn at the initial community meeting, wanting the windows installed, but when the reverend put it out there so clearly, she could not remember her argument for keeping the windows. He was right, they were a distraction.

She still had two more years to enjoy them. That was when the building of the new Fort Angus IBS was set for completion. The land had been bought, the renderings of the squat cinder-block building made public, and the funds were being raised. Lyddy Compton herself had responded to the reverend's call for support. "Why deed your assets to people you claim as family, but who are not part of the Lord's family?"

When the reverend put it that way, it made perfect sense, just like with the windows. It made sense to others, too, as Lyddy watched a hundred heads nodding in unison.

Fort Angus Imperial Baptist Sanctuary was not the largest Imperial Baptist church in the coalition, but it was among the most active. In fact, within the past ten years the IBS had chartered a school, elected four of the eight town officials, and was the second-biggest investor at the Fort Angus Savings Bank.

Bob Jones University, a bastion of moral education in these end times, said the reverend, had underwritten the start-up costs for the new school, and Lyddy thought wistfully about the programming. She wished it had been an option for Phil and Miles, but for her daughter-in-law, Rosemary, especially. Rosemary would have benefited from a decent, moral education.

The pews of the old church were polished maple, scratched, but clean. Each pew held at least four bodies, and Lyddy checked them off from her position as organist. She knew every single individual in the church, knew their families, and knew their history. She was feeling very pleased at the late-summer turnout until she watched Christine and Paul Delfino walk in through the heavy door.

Lyddy continued to play the welcoming hymns, but she dropped a note when Christine and Paul took the third pew from the front. The entire congregation knew that was the Angus family pew, and Lyddy felt disgusted that the Delfino family would do such a blatant thing. Where was Karen Angus expected to sit now?

Christine and Paul Delfino had attended services for five Sundays in a row, always choosing a different and wrong place to sit. Lyddy did not know why they even bothered. At first, she thought they might be making fun of the church. Then, the second time, she suspected they were high. Now, on the fifth Sunday, Lyddy didn't know what to make of them.

"They've gone and found religion," Nellie Ballou told Ada during a visit to the nursing home. It was one of Nellie's lucid days, and she was downright pissed off that her daughter Christine had come by spouting about hellfire and Nellie's soul. In fact, Nellie had pitched the large-print Bible at Christine's head, but she was quick and ducked before it made impact.

When she heard about the scene at the nursing home, Ada called up the third Ballou sister, Joyce, and told her that it wasn't right to harass their mother in such a fragile state, and that she wasn't having it. For all she cared, she said, Christine could shove that Bible straight up her fat ass. She hollered into the telephone until Joyce began to cry. Disgusted, Ada hung up, and Joyce drove the ten miles across town to Christine's farmhouse to make peace.

Christine told Joyce that for her whole life she'd been a sinner and done some vile, vile things, but she was getting right with Jesus now. Christine motioned for Joyce to sit down at the kitchen table, loaded up with old papers and dirty dishes. Christine said she was making it her personal mission to see that Nellie made it to heaven, and couldn't Joyce see that was the right thing to do?

Joyce nodded and said she understood, that she'd talk to Ada once she cooled down, and she agreed to take a notice home for Sunday services. Joyce promised she'd mention it to Drew, but as she drove back toward town, she knew the last thing she wanted was to sit for services at the Fort Angus Imperial Baptist Sanctuary.

"Can you believe they wore jeans to church?" Karen Angus said as she smoked her little cigarette behind the church kitchen and Lyddy Compton nodded in sympathy. The two women assessed Christine and Paul Delfino. Christine's shoes were pink canvas while Paul wore work boots, mustard colored and scuffed.

"Why do they even bother?" Lyddy responded.

Karen shrugged.

Christine was one of the last to leave after the service, and she offered to clean up, but Karen gave her a big hug and told her not to be silly. Lyddy smiled and did the same. When Christine left, both Karen and Lyddy scraped the platter remains into the garbage bin and dumped the cold coffee from the urn into the sink, astounded that Christine did not insist.

"Sure, she offered," Karen said as she wiped down the church kitchen counters, "but you can just tell she didn't mean it."

Lyddy nodded, remembering Christine Ballou from high school. Lyddy was a little older than Ada and Christine and a lot older than Joyce, but she clearly recalled the two oldest Ballous behind the brick walls, standing in a circle of other dirty people. Lyddy remembered the whole group of them, all denim-clad, greasy, and stinking of cigarette smoke. She'd been afraid to walk the shortcut past the back stairs when the Ballou sisters were leaning on the railings. Lyddy had walked all the way around the school to the front entrance in order to avoid them, her eyes forward and intent as she gripped her book satchel with a tight fist. To this day, Lyddy resented that extra loop.

The Ballous, in their black eyeliner, ironed hair, and heavy mascara, were trash, dropping out, both getting pregnant by God knows who. And when they were gone, nobody in the school missed them. That was a natural fact, thought Lyddy. Nobody missed them at Homecoming, or the Potato Blossom Festival, or at any of the ball games. The Ballous checked out of every important event at Fort Angus High School, and for her part, Lyddy was glad.

Karen Angus read her mind, and nodded. "Trashy," she said.

Although, the two women conceded as they sponged down the community tables, Joyce Ballou was all right. But, Karen pointed out, "Joyce married a Freid, so she's a Freid now."

11

MILES COMPTON SPENDS TIME AT THE NURSING HOME.

*T*he Fort Angus Rescue Farm was overrun with cats. It was overrun with dogs, too, but luckily, it housed only one old brown horse. Built as a clapboard addition on the old Kinkead farmstead, it was intended to house fifty stray and abandoned animals, but twice as many now roamed the facility. Cats on the filing cabinets, cats under the desk, and one new-arrival dog chased a cat from the staff chair when Lyddy Compton knocked on the door. For thirty years, Lyddy kept the building smelling nice. Each morning after she wiped down her own kitchen countertops, she'd make the drive across town and up the hill to the farm's office. She'd cleaned cages, kennels, and the horse stall so often, Lyddy felt more relaxed at the rescue farm than she did in her own space.

It started as a way to get out of the house, to do something with those lonely morning hours when Phil was at school and the mayor was working, before Miles was born. She cleaned and re-cleaned her house on those mornings, each piece of furniture placed just so, each ornament with no trace of dust. Her home felt hollow on those mornings before she found the farm, and she used to stand with her long thin arms dangling, her mind useless and caged.

The mayor said absolutely no animals in the house when Lyddy brought it up. Absolutely not, he'd said, and Lyddy took his word as truth.

But, Lyddy had grown up on a New Brunswick farm. She'd been raised with sheep and cows and an old border collie that slept in the barn. The barn cats were too many to number, and she remembered her parents telling her that where there were cats, there were no rats.

Lyddy thought about her cat-free home, then caught an image of the mayor as a rat. The image made her giggle out loud, and that is how she got the idea to volunteer for the Fort Angus Rescue Farm.

The owners of the farm had changed over several times, but the soap in her pail was a constant for Lyddy. She enjoyed the warm water on her hands, enjoyed the satisfaction of sponging out the cages each morning. It was almost as if she was bathing each animal directly, the way she imagined it.

"There, there," she said in her head. "Now doesn't that feel nice?"

While she scooped and sponged, the cats would rub necks against her bent legs. Sometimes, one cat would be more persistent than the others, pushing its face into Lyddy's elbow and demanding that Lyddy remove her yellow gloves and take a moment to scratch its kitty chin.

Even though Lyddy had shoveled manure from the horse stalls for more than thirty years, and even though her husband was the former mayor, her son Miles was not allowed to apply for the part-time position.

"Lyddy, we just can't take the chance." The reverend told her this in the staff kitchen as he pushed a sleeping cat from the countertop. The reverend sat down at the table with his cup, having just that week been deeded the farm as a bequest to the church. "Kids come in here all the time, and what if he did something to one of them?"

Like what, Lyddy wanted to ask, but she stood tight-lipped against the wall. Her son liked to be with men, she thought, but she could not find a way of saying those words out loud in a way that felt right.

Yes, Lyddy wanted to say out loud to the reverend, her son's photo was on that state website, but there was a difference between straight-up rape and consensual acts. Her son liked to be with one particular student, three years younger. It wasn't rape if the person said yes. And, that boy had said yes. That boy had said yes, Lyddy thought bitterly, wondering why Miles had not called to ask for her help. He just signed papers from that boy's parents.

Miles signed the papers, and now he was on the pervert website as a homosexual and a statutory rapist. Lyddy struggled to even think that word about her son, but homosexual came easier than rapist. Homosexual, yes. Rapist, no.

Miles had been told no at McDonald's, at the mill, at the

glove factory, at the nursing home, and the animal shelter. The no from Phil had been the most difficult to take.

"Absolutely not," Phil spoke in a mandate, and Lyddy was struck at how similar Phil was to his father. Lyddy knew she should speak up and insist on filing, telephones, research, just something to help her youngest son. But, in the presence of Phil's determination, she backed down. She overheard him talking to Rosemary outside the garage.

"Can you believe she wants me to bring Miles into the office?"

While his father was oblivious to any speculation, Phil Compton was not. Even though he was just a teenager when his little brother had been born, Phil had heard the rumors throughout the halls of Fort Angus High School. It wasn't so obvious when Miles was a baby, but as he grew, Phil compared photos. Phil was a mini-version of the mayor, but to anyone with eyes, Miles was a Pratt, and that fact made his own mother a slut.

Rosemary nodded at her husband with her hands on her hips and her jaw dropped way down. Rosemary's mother, Karen Angus, had told her about Miles being on the pervert website, but Rosemary had to see for herself. Sure enough, she told Phil, there was Miles' photo. And now Lyddy wanted a state-certified pervert working with Phil? What if Miles went on a raping spree right there in the lobby, she whispered to Phil. What then? Rosemary watched the television, and she knew things like that happened.

For his part, Miles kept quiet. He slept in his room, and up until the week before, washed and dressed his father each morning while Lyddy bustled about the house before leaving for the animal shelter, avoiding eye contact with either of them.

Last week, Miles packed his father's belongings. The mayor was allowed one small suitcase of personal items, and he insisted those items include a cosmetics bag and a formal evening gown. Miles indulged the request, but when it was time to make the drive, he quietly substituted a box stacked neatly with comfortable clothing and slippers, toothpaste, and a folder of magazines.

He visited the mayor every afternoon since the move, making sure to bring copies of the newspapers, both the *Bangor Daily News* and the weekly *Fort Angus Republican*. These visits went well, considering that his father had difficulty recognizing Miles and the staff refused to look him directly in the face.

Miles walked through the door deliberately, with his head up. He nodded to the receptionist. He'd made a habit of visiting daily, and even though he'd been told, icily, that he could not volunteer in an official capacity, there was no rule that said a pervert couldn't visit his own father.

Since Miles had a clear, teacher's reading voice, the other residents gathered around his chair. Ms. Nellie Ballou, especially, liked to scoot her wheelchair in close. She was older than Mayor Compton, but they had matching dementia diagnoses, and so when Miles arrived after lunch each day for the afternoon, the mayor pushed Ms. Nellie's chair down the long, slick hallway toward the visiting area.

With a degree of ceremony, Mayor Compton would straighten Ms. Nellie's chair, fix the afghan on her lap, and then settle into the cushioned bench beside her. He leaned forward, as if on a listening campaign. With elbow on knee and chin in hand, he nodded as Miles read the newspapers, cover to cover.

During a particularly emotional story, the mayor placed his hand on Ms. Nellie's arm, and Ms. Nellie smiled up at Mayor Compton. When Miles finished and left, the staff exhaled. Miles noticed the nurses pacing the doorway of the visiting room, their eyes fixed with anticipation, wondering what Miles might do next.

Half the staff was hoping he'd expose himself to the residents, as the days tended to stretch with nothing interesting in between the hours. The other half just wanted Miles to leave. "He gives me the creeps," one of the afternoon girls said. "He does. He just does."

When Miles made ready to stand and leave each day, Ms. Nellie took hold of his wrist and pulled him close with her single, functional hand. She patted his shoulder and kissed his cheek. "Thank you," she said. "You're a good boy." She said this and nodded in the direction of Mayor Compton. "He's a good boy."

For her part, Nellie Ballou was an original County Girl. There was a black-and-white photograph on her bedside table, taken in the early forties. Miles noticed this photo in its cheap metal frame the day he found his father in her room, asking to borrow a pair of pantyhose. He was just about to reach for his father's elbow and lead him back down the hallway and into his own bedroom when he saw the photograph.

A young Nellie was perched on a wooden bench with a backdrop of paper flowers, wearing lipstick and smiling. Her dress was filmy, fashionable, and just a little bit risqué with its provocative neckline. Miles looked from Ms. Nellie, bent forward in her wheelchair, to the photo and then back again.

The photo, while lovely, did not convey the fact that Nellie, as the daughter of an immigrant French Canadian family, was the first Ballou born in the United States. Miles could not know that Nellie's birth had caused the death of her mother. And then her father. Christine says from grief, but Ada thinks liquor.

Miles was unaware that Nellie's parents deeded the garrison hill farmhouse to their boys, who raised her as best they could until they, too, died off one by one—Claude in the war, John in a fight, and Rene on the train tracks. At fifteen, Nellie started work at Mr. Kinkead's café, which was, before it burned down, connected to the Sunrise Cinema. The Café was actually a stripped-down soda fountain that sold meat-loaf sandwiches and sliced ham for a nickel.

Beside the photo of Nellie on the moon, Miles saw another silver-framed photograph of her entertaining some soldiers at the old café counter. The ribbon in her hair was tied into a fat bow, and her dress was hitched up to show her knees as she sat square on a soldier's lap.

Miles smiled, but he did not know that during the war, soldiers were stationed at the garrison, and when Nellie's growing belly appeared a year later, the soldiers were blamed.

Of course, it didn't help Nellie's reputation that she continued to entertain the garrison soldiers at the farmhouse throughout her pregnancy. She used to ride through downtown Fort Angus with her big belly, a soldier on each side ready to light her next cigarette.

"That girl," the Angus and Compton and Kinkead ladies all nodded. "Trashy." The Angus and Compton and Kinkead ladies clicked on and on about Nellie's red lipstick. They also talked about her curly red hair, which she kept long and shiny. "Oh Nellie, you should braid that hair back," she was told by the brand-new Mrs. Kinkead as she stepped out of her freshly washed blue convertible.

Two months pregnant, not yet showing, but full of hormones, Nellie told the young Mrs. Kinkead to take her bullshit comments and shove them up her dimpled white ass. She said the words in French, but she stared hard at Mr. Kinkead when she said them. This was how Nellie lost her job at the Fort Angus Café, but it was also how she received cash in an envelope every week from Mr. Kinkead until he died.

Miles Compton knew none of these details when he led his father from Ms. Nellie's room on the day Ms. Nellie told him she had no pantyhose to lend him. Miles had apologized to Nellie's daughter, Christine, there with a Bible, and then walked his father across the hall.

Miles recalled the photo of Ms. Nellie each time he watched her sit beside his father. He thought about a young Nellie with her dress hitched up to her knees, reputation be damned, as he read to the small crowd gathered in the sun-filled activity room. He thought about the difference between then and now, and he wondered how his own life would eventually set and who, if anyone, would read newspapers to him.

It was a stupid mistake, he thought, replaying the details of his crime out in his mind, and he winced. It was a dumb mistake. Seventeen was too young, and Miles, at twenty, should have known as much. He maintained his wincing expression until, as she did every day, Ms. Nellie looked at him and drew him close with her good hand. Miles wanted so badly to believe Ms. Nellie was lucid when she kissed his cheek and said, as always, that he was a good, good boy.

12

Rhetta thinks about Fort Angus history and potato fields.

$\mathcal{S}$till in the car, lost in a mishmash of recollection, Rhetta passed Bangor, and she moved her shoulders up and down to loosen the muscles. Two hours into the drive, she watched the Orono turnoff with its highway sign indicating only 120 more miles to Fort Angus. The highway was now a straight asphalt line, cut through the center of rough granite ledges.

Had she been traveling with someone, any conversation would have yielded to silence when the towns got sparse and the first signs advertised "T2-R7" and then "T2-R4," literal geological map coordinates. Even though the morning sun shined brightly through the windshield, it was easy to doze, and she reminded herself to stay alert.

Rhetta leaned her head on the car window and watched the treetops blur—their branches grabbing up toward the empty blue sky. The radio cut down to three stations, and the two clearest were a conservative talk show and contemporary Christian music. These stations were short blips of sound as they were picked up by the radio scanner—digital station numbers flashing by over and over again. With her mind on autopilot, Rhetta glided along the highway, thinking less about the frequent "Danger: Moose Crossing" signs and more about the idea of coming home.

The founder of Fort Angus, Silas Angus, was an Army colonel and, accompanied by his eight children—including a daughter-in-law who was married just the day before the trip—set off from Massachusetts in the summer of 1807.

As she drove, Rhetta imagined the girl's honeymoon—slogging through weeks of mud and forest and river with her new in-laws. If the trip is tedious in a car, the thought of making it by ship, and then riverboat, and then canoe, and then by horse-drawn wagon loaded down with family in the most primitive conditions—mud-rutted and full of blackflies—was positively unbearable. After two months, resting only briefly at loose Canadian townships along the interior route, the Angus family finally stopped short at the rough New Brunswick border.

What would become Lupine Mountain loomed to the north, the gray Abnaki River at their feet. Blue sky ran for miles in each direction, and despite the sweat and dirt in their clothing, Rhetta imagined the air smelled clean. The Anguses were home.

Rhetta imagined the travelers sighed with relieved and tired faces, hands on hips, and looked around them. Legend held that on an earlier scouting mission, Colonel Silas Angus befriended a young Micmac guide. It is written that the Micmac guide extended his hand in good faith and told Silas Angus in perfect English, "I will show you good land."

This legend is engraved on a plaque bolted into a large rock memorial at the old Fort Angus Garrison. It also figured prominently in the 200-year-anniversary celebration of the town's founding. The local community theater group, sponsored by the Baptist church, reenacted the scene with Colonel Angus and the Micmac guide and, despite the well-attended public showing of the film at the Sunrise Cinema, Rhetta doubted the history was one hundred percent accurate.

After watching the video of the theater's performance, Rhetta wanted to ask her mother if it made any sense for a Native American scout to freely offer up his homeland to white strangers with guns. She also wanted to ask if it made sense that a Native American scout would speak such eloquent English, but Rhetta remained silent. She knew Ada would ask her why she couldn't just say "Indian" like everyone else, and why she had to set herself apart, and why she thought she was so much better than everyone else.

Rhetta knew all this because Ada had slapped her face once when she'd said "dinner" instead of "supper." It was a simple twist, said on a visit home from college, but Ada got mad. Rhetta thought of that slap, and she thought of how fierce Ada's expression had been when she told her they said supper, not dinner, and for her to never forget where she came from.

"Ever," Ada had repeated in two distinct syllables, one inch from Rhetta's stinging cheek.

On their arrival in 1807, Silas Angus and his family had no way of knowing that their town would later be judged the shire town, or county seat, before the honor was eventually given over to Houlton, with its more prominent location. He had no idea that his arrival would further displace three different tribes of Native Americans—the Abnaki, Maliseet, and Micmac. He could not foretell that in fifty years Fort Angus would boast Maine's first Canadian–American railroad crossing, or that the advent of the Bangor and Aroostook Railroad would bring a level of industry and commerce that remains unduplicated: two colleges, a dance pavilion, military base, and a booming timber and farming industry.

Neither Angus nor Kinkead nor the eventual Comptons predicted this early industry would lead to the creation of some exquisite homes. A ride through Fort Angus's downtown is an architectural history lesson, and when describing her hometown, Rhetta struggled with the contrasts.

In the blocks immediately circling the downtown proper are expansive Victorian homes—large, impressive structures with intricate cookie-cutter woodwork and multiple cupolas. These homes line both sides of Main Street, River Street, and Depot Lane. Some are well-maintained, parts of former estates that sprawl a half block or more, while others have been chopped into multi-unit, low-income apartment buildings. In their heyday, these houses symbolized a level of wealth and prosperity typical of the pioneering folks up from Massachusetts, hoping to mold a new Boston.

But now the industry that supported these homes is gone. The college went bankrupt in 1972 when the war ended and the call for border-town colleges dropped. The railroad no longer operates. The site of the garrison hill barracks is a park now, and little children climb up replicas of former training installations, barely noticing the plaque depicting the town's historical significance. A family from out of state uses the old dance pavilion as a summer camp.

Even the loggers have trouble, and Joyce's husband Drew Freid struggled with tedious state regulations and expensive equipment that can't be maintained with a logger's salary. The farmers are still there, the hardiest have dug into the earth and cling to their family roots. And families, especially the old fixtures, have endured just like the buildings.

Rhetta supposed Silas Angus would be proud of this legacy. As she drove farther and farther north along the highway, past ripe potato fields on both sides of her car, she pictured the potato harvest each September and October. It wasn't until she left Fort Angus that she learned it was strange for a school to close during potato-harvest season. For three weeks each year, children worked in the fields.

Imagine, Rhetta said, describing the scene to her friends and colleagues, a patchwork of square dirt fields laid out in parallel rows, thick pine trees banking the far corners. Each picker is given a section of row and a wide-mouthed basket. The digger truck lumbers up and down the rows, turning over the soil and exposing the potatoes like seashells or rocks on a narrow beach. The picker's job is to keep up, removing the potatoes before the digger cycles back. Kids picked across the field from right to left in tandem for three weeks each fall, waiting for a truck to collect the full barrels.

Her stepfather, Clint, Rhetta explained, worked the truck with the other men: big bearded men in heavy hooded sweatshirts with torn pockets, each manning a rusty grappling crane. Their hooks swung the barrels of freshly picked potatoes up from the field to the flatbed. Clint released each barrel and rolled it neatly into a row with the others. When it was placed, he removed a paper ticket from the edge and stuck it into a dirty envelope inside his shirt.

The guys on the barrel truck were paid by the hour. Pickers were paid by the ticket. Pickers tagged a full barrel of potatoes with a printed slip of paper bearing their assigned number. At the end of the day, the field boss collected these grubby ticket envelopes from the men, separating them and logging each stack into a book for payment: fifty cents a ticket.

What Rhetta did not detail was that Ada Ballou had married Clint in the Fort Angus courthouse not long after Lamen Hollander shot himself. After Clint moved in, Ada volleyed each day with a "Could you just give him a break?" to her daughter, and a "Could you just ease up?" to Clint. The new baby was a surprise to everyone.

One harvest morning, Ada stood in Rhetta's bedroom doorway, baby on her hip. "Up, up," she called as the electric light burned Rhetta's eyes. The kitchen radio was already broadcasting a static-filled potato picker's special: "The time is 4:05, and we've got an update for all you folks who might be concerned about the weather. Got that list, Mike?"

Mike Smith's grainy voice ran down the names of local farmers, and Rhetta listened with anticipation from the comfort of her blankets. "Jewell's is a go this morning. Fitzpatrick's is running an hour late—that's one hour late, folks. They're trying to fix a broken truck. Repeat—one hour late for Graham Fitzpatrick. Porter's crew is a go. Rainier's is a go."

When the list was finished, and Frank Rainier's crew was called on time, Rhetta crawled out of the covers, stomping disappointment with her bare feet on the clapboard floors. The kitchen was warm when she entered, but she rubbed her hands together out of habit.

Ada had gone back to bed with the baby, but two gallon-sized plastic milk jugs stood filled on the table, one held tap water and the other grape Kool-Aid. Clint finished his cup of coffee at the table and waited, smoking a cigarette and flipping though the *Uncle Henry's Swap-and-Sell-it Guide*. Clint held his empty mug with one hand by the rim, as if it was Styrofoam instead of a thick ceramic mug, while Rhetta stared at him from the kitchen counter, gulping her own hot coffee and shoving lunch into a paper bag.

"Ready?" he said, looking up from the booklet.

She shrugged.

She was eleven years old, and they were meant to be in the field by five.

Clint had warmed up the truck, but the cold from the vinyl seat shot through Rhetta's layers. The radio station advertised coffee and eggs at the Miss Angus Diner for a farmer's breakfast, and Rhetta sat back, resting her dirty boots on the edges of the milk jugs.

"Think it'll rain today?" Clint asked.

She shrugged again, silent.

When he dropped her at the edge of the field that morning, she grunted "thanks," and slammed the door. It was still dark, and she struggled to find the field boss from the small group of shadowy people gathered around a pile of empty barrels. The rows were crunchy under her feet, the earth stiff from the frost, potato tops cracking as she walked. She carried a jug in each hand, her lunch bag tucked under an arm. Her nose ran, and she wished she'd packed a length of toilet paper as she wiped an awkward cuff across her face.

The field boss was a plump lady named Bev with a clipboard, and she assigned sections to the crowd of children. When Rhetta approached, she gestured with her thumb to keep walking toward the far, far end of the field.

Rhetta's field section was approximately twenty feet, between Emmett Pratt and Rosemary Angus. Emmett was fine to work beside, but Rosemary had a million brothers and cousins in the same field, and every day they lobbed rotten potatoes across the rows at each other or played tricks like peeing into an empty bottle and offering it to Emmett, telling him it was lemonade. Rosemary and her Angus and Compton cousins horded rotten potatoes in little piles, and when they threw them, the white slime seeped out midair, falling in strings on everything within the trajectory. Rotten potatoes smell exactly like dog shit and tomato vomit, and the stink stayed on a glove or shoulder for days.

Sometimes they stole tickets from other kids' full barrels and replaced them with their own before the truck arrived. The Angus and Compton families wore brand new flannel shirts and clean blue jeans to the field each day.

Rhetta had been to the Angus house once, for Rosemary's birthday party. The entire class was invited, and Rhetta made herself dizzy walking up and down their spiral staircase while the other kids fixed orange soda in the kitchen from a machine that used syrup and compressed air in a can. Mrs. Karen Angus sat rigid on a fancy pink couch, smoking thin little cigarettes. She sat there the whole afternoon, except once, when she grabbed Rhetta's arm and pulled her off the staircase. She looked at Rhetta hard and said that a woman could never be too rich or too thin. The whole Angus family made her nervous, and Rhetta was jealous that Bev assigned Emmett an end section with only the pine trees as border.

For two hours, the kids picked in the dark, fingers freezing despite their work gloves. Rhetta placed her basket behind the potatoes, hunkered over, and began lightly tossing them in, edging up the length of the row until the basket was full. Then she lugged it to an empty barrel with two straining arms. She dumped it over, leaning slightly on the chest-high edge of the barrel as the potatoes cascaded down. She repeated the process until the barrel was full and the row picked clean.

As the sun rose, they became dark figures on the horizon, taking on a golden and glowing silhouette. There was no chatter, just the repeating thud of potatoes landing. It was mind-numbing, digging for potatoes in the half-frozen fields, and she was grateful when a car with out-of-state plates pulled to the side of the road. A lady in a red coat stepped from the door, her camera pointed at them.

This often happened during the harvest. There could be as many as three cars lined up on the shoulder, watching the fieldwork as vehicles idled with heaters running. Sometimes people got out of their cars and asked to buy a basket, tightly handwoven by Elmore Savoy as part of a contract with his family and others in the Micmac tribe. When crews were photographed, those pictures often ended up on a tourist display or posted in a Maine travel guide.

Many years later, Rhetta saw a calendar of the Aroostook County potato harvest in an airport bookstore. The pictures were exquisite, all peaceful and industrious and golden at early sunrise. But the pictures did not show dirty faces, or a child reaching down for a potato and sticking a hand into a rotten one—oozing white slime—and then puking from the rancid odor. There were no stooped shoulders or muddy boots.

Rhetta watched the lady in the red coat as she stood straddled over the potato row, freshly dug, dust sticking to her jeans,
basket in hand. The woman in the red coat kneeled into the
gravel on the side of the road, and Rhetta heard the click of
the camera shutter repeat a dozen more times. Then the lady
snapped her camera into its case and opened the door to her
warm, still idling car. When the car door opened, Rhetta heard
the sound of music just before the door shut. A few seconds
later, the car was gone.

At that moment, Rhetta wanted to be that lady. With a
clean red coat and the means to just drive away, she represented something hopeful. Rhetta didn't know it then, but
she represented the idea of choice: that she could one day
choose to pick the potatoes, or she could choose to drive away.
The lady in the red coat with her camera hanging around her
neck had planted the beginning of a thought in her mind,
that there might be more for Rhetta in late September than
this field. Like an itch, this half-formed thought traveled in
her eleven-year-old brain until the hum and tubercular cough
of the digger truck in the distance eventually drowned it out.
Rhetta bent over to fill her basket before the digger truck
rumbled back.

It was hot by mid-morning and Rhetta tossed her jacket
toward the milk jugs that marked the end of her section. By
lunchtime, she was picking in only a T-shirt. Her bare arms were

dusty, and the potato dirt mixed with sweat made a brown paste on her forehead.

The Kool-Aid was nearly gone, and the water jug was streaked with mud from the combination of condensation and grimy hands. When Bev blew the whistle for lunch and the truck engines went idle, Rhetta emptied the basket and sat on the pile of clothing.

She took off her gloves and wiped the dust from her hands on the front of her shirt. Emmett sat down beside her.

"What're you going to do with your money?" he asked, opening up her lunch bag.

"School clothes," Rhetta said. "You?"

"Maybe save it."

They watched Rosemary finish her lunch early and then throw a wad of gum into her younger brother's hair. He howled and began to chase her with a pus-filled potato.

"Damn, that smells," yelled an older boy from down the row. "Cut the crap, Rosemary."

Rhetta rubbed her shoulder and twisted it around in circles. Sitting had made it stiffen up and get sore. Soon Clint came by to see if she needed more water.

"No thanks," she mumbled, squinting up at him from the ground, and after a minute of awkward silence, an apple in his hand, he walked back to eat with the men.

Returning to work after lunch was a slow process, and she fought the urge to ask Bev for a shorter section or just go lay down.

Bend and pick. Bend and pick. She'd picked roughly twenty barrels a day for the past three days, so that meant $10 a day for the full six-day work week—$60 before taxes. Multiply that by the three weeks school was let out for the harvest, and she had almost $200 of take-home pay for nearly a month's work.

As she picked, she mapped out the route she'd walk into town, even though when she mentioned it to Ada, Clint offered her a ride. Ada stood beside him and bore a "please do this for me" look. Neither Clint nor Rhetta could determine which of them the look was meant for.

"I can drop you off if you want."

She shrugged.

As the sun went down, it became difficult to see the potatoes, and Rhetta tripped over rocks as she dragged her milk jugs and jacket from row to row. Her fingers were gritty and dry from the dirt. She coughed, watching her breath in the near darkness. She was shivering in all her layers and she hoped the barrel she'd just filled would be the last of the day.

When Bev blew the whistle to walk back, Rhetta looked around at what they'd done. The field behind them was picked empty, the rows mashed down from feet and truck wheels. The field in front—the next day's project—was high and ripe. The kids walked tiredly, huddled in jackets with baskets dangling to one side, filled with old lunch sacks and dirty gloves. Bev hollered from ahead and asked if anyone needed extra tickets made for the morning.

By the time the pickers walked to the road, the men had already finished unloading the barrels into the potato houses. Clint sat in the pickup waiting for Rhetta, the orange tip of his cigarette a stark contrast to the dark truck cab. She opened the door and climbed up stiffly.

"How'd you do?" he asked, tossing the butt through the window and pulling the gear shift.

At that moment in the warm truck, staring straight through the windshield down the dark, dirt road ahead, Rhetta had no words to articulate that she was tired. She was tired from the physical work, but it was bigger than sore muscles. She saw only another day in the field tomorrow, after another night in their cluttered family farmhouse. She couldn't formulate, much less say out loud, that she was beginning to see this daily routine as the blueprint of family life, of her life—that there would be nothing more than these fields, these swollen knuckles, this long day. She had no word for "uninspired," or the belief that her mind was meant for something different.

Because she had no words for these emotions, she couldn't yet process the converse: that this life was a choice for many in the northern Maine community, that it had merit and taught, among other things, the value of work and people and money. She had no idea that as an adult, she might be proud and grateful for the potato-picking experience, this ride home with her stepfather.

Since she lacked the complexity to see it as a choice, she only felt a longing for something different, for things to be different somehow. The idea of choice—a career, family, where she lived, anything—was as foreign to Rhetta as the lady in the red coat, with her camera and out-of-state plates.

So when Clint and Rhetta drove home that night and he asked her how she did, Rhetta just kicked at the empty milk jugs.

"Nothing special."

13

RHETTA REGRETS DATING A MARRIED MAN.

*A*s Rhetta Ballou tried to stuff the open space in her mind during the drive with thoughts of the physical: potato dirt, potato-blossom queens, and new-potato suppers, she avoided thoughts of the emotional. She avoided those thoughts until she passed the green highway sign marking the Aroostook County line.

Rhetta had never considered dating an older man, but the Fort Angus High School cafeteria was a dismal place, all mint-colored cinderblock, even with first-day-of-school energy and hum. Without Wendy Jo there to mock the stupid things about Rosemary Angus, or Emmett Pratt to smile at her from the back row, it was just a foul-smelling place to break up the day. So, while Wendy Jo was newly married and expecting her first baby, and Emmett Pratt was starting life as a full-time employee, an equally teenaged Rhetta got permission to eat her lunch, not in the cabbage-scented cafeteria, but in the history classroom with Mr. Bates.

The classroom windows looked out over open fields leading toward the churning Abnaki River behind the school. On a clear day, Rhetta could see little silver glimpses of water and the outline of the bridge.

"No ring?" Mr. Bates opened the door on the first day, alluding to the gossip from when Phil Compton took her to the prom last June.

It was just a few months ago, but Mr. Bates recalled Rhetta's quiet response to the class chatter and innuendo. She just scooted lower into her desk seat and opened a book. Her cousin Wendy Jo was the one who stood up and told Rosemary Angus to go fuck herself sideways.

"No ring." Rhetta held up her hand as evidence.

She opened her sandwich and licked peanut butter from the edges of the bread, stretching her legs across an empty chair. Mr. Bates rummaged in his desk drawer and removed a plastic dish.

"Leftovers," he said, gesturing to the cold chicken inside.

Rhetta assessed Mr. Bates. Big, gray eyes. Dark hair. Tall. Khaki pants and a white collared shirt. No tie. Mr. Bates had been the history teacher for two years, and his energetic and earnest face was a contrast to the pallid expressions of other teachers at Fort Angus High. Rosemary Angus bragged that she could fuck Mr. Bates any time she wanted, but Wendy Jo called that bullshit one day in the locker room.

"I could fuck any of the men in this town, if I wanted." Rosemary said, pouting in the mirror and inspecting her lipstick.

"How about you go fuck yourself," Wendy Jo said, standing behind Rosemary and meeting her eyes in the wall-length mirror.

Rosemary could not think of words quick enough, so Wendy Jo grabbed Rhetta's arm to leave.

Rhetta remembered the way Wendy Jo's hand felt on her arm, and Rhetta felt protected. Now, eating her lunch in front of Mr. Bates, Rhetta felt herself wishing that Mr. Bates would put his hand on her arm, too. When Mr. Bates told Rhetta he was twenty four, and she called him an old man, Mr. Bates clutched at his chest in mock protest, and she smiled.

For the rest of August and into September, Rhetta spent every lunch hour in the history classroom. The principal told Mr. Bates it was a good thing for him to spend extra time with Rhetta, given her family background, and she could use a mentor. She overheard him say as much, and still reeling from Phil Compton's words, she assumed she needed a mentor because her family was poor. Although, after hearing Nellie once call Principal Evan Kelly the man with the shortest dick in Aroostook County, Rhetta would later wonder if he was operating on a more sinister suggestion.

On one particular day, after a winter of lunches, Mr. Bates offered Rhetta a slice of his green apple. But this time, instead of taking it from his outstretched palm, she took the slice of apple from his hand with her teeth, dragging the slice from the center of his palm down the length of his index finger and then lifting it with her tongue into her mouth in a single motion.

"Party trick," she said, in between bites before she swallowed.

"Indeed," said Mr. Bates.

Mr. Bates bought Rhetta a journal. Its cover showed a picture of a lighthouse downstate in Portland, the red-topped roof against blue ocean and bluer sky beyond. The paper was smooth and white, and Rhetta hesitated before first putting her cheap Bic against it. This was the first time she ever wrote anything down that wasn't a list or a note to Wendy Jo or answers to a test or a class assignment. She hesitated, nervous and unsure.

She remembered those details in her car, two minutes past the Aroostook County line and a half hour from home. She remembered the journal and the apple and Mr. Bates' leftover chicken lunch on that first day. It felt important to Rhetta because like that night in the car with Phil Compton, the act of putting pen to paper marked the beginning of something big for her. Like the night with Phil, it was another moment where, if Rhetta could, she would reach across time and face her younger self.

She would stand toe to toe and ask that girl precisely what she thought she was doing. She would tell her to thank Mr. Bates for the journal but to walk out that door. But she'd just turned sixteen, her best friend was pregnant, and her other friend was pumping gas full-time, and she knew enough about sex to feel like she knew it all. "Mrs. Rhetta Bates," she wrote in scrawly penmanship on the first page of the journal. Over and over.

Mr. Bates also bought her a leather jacket, and when Ada questioned the gift, she brushed it off.

"He's my friend."

"You know he's married, don't you?" Rhetta did not know this, but she steeled her face and blinked back at her mother.

"And he's expecting a baby."

At that moment the kitchen started to spin. She had never thought to ask Mr. Bates if he was married, let alone if his wife was expecting a baby. She took off the jacket.

Just the day before, Rhetta had stroked the hair behind his ears and asked if he wanted her to call him by his first name. He shook his head no, so she kept repeating "Mr. Bates. Mr. Bates. Mr. Bates."

The day Ada told her about Vera Bates, Rhetta turned up at Nellie's old farmhouse. Nellie saw her on the steps, muddy and frantic, and immediately sent her out for Salem Ultra Lights and coffee brandy. While Nellie poured the brandy into the milk with ice, she put her hand on Rhetta's shoulder. Her voice was raspy.

"Don't you cry, Rhetta," she warned. "Don't you dare cry."

And that was all she said until after they'd watched *The Edge of Night*. Rhetta carried in plastic tumblers, and the two women smoked menthols on a threadbare and faded velvet couch for the entire afternoon.

Mr. Bates backpedaled when Rhetta confronted him with the information. They walked the Abnaki shoreline, and Rhetta threw the leather jacket at his feet. It was early spring by then, and she shivered in short sleeves.

"Just put the jacket on, Rhetta." Mr. Bates started to cry. Rhetta walked ahead of him, and she turned when she heard his choking sounds. He had dropped to his knees, and the moist, muddy ground seeped wet patches on his pants.

Rhetta had never seen a man cry before, and his expression was twisted into features that would look mean if there were no tears on his cheeks. She thought about kicking him. She thought about high-kicking him square in his face.

She still wasn't a hundred percent sure that she would not kick his face, but Mr. Bates grabbed her waist and pressed his head into her belly. His hair was tangled in her fingers and her mind was on the grown man there before her on his knees. Rhetta stood this way, with her back to the path and her hands in his hair, and didn't see Vera Bates lumbering by the shoreline, eight months pregnant in a denim jumper. "Vera?" Mr. Bates stood up. "You want him, Rhetta?" Vera Bates pointed her finger toward her husband.

"You want him?" she said louder, and Rhetta's mouth hung low.

Rhetta wished she could say that Vera Bates hauled off and slapped her. She wished she could say that Vera slapped her so hard her body spun down, that her jeans were permanently stained and that she still carried a scar on her leg from landing so hard in the wet gravel shoreline, cut on an old wire or piece of glass.

That would have purged her, Rhetta thought in her car as her breathing got shallower and shallower with the memory. An act of revenge would have reset some karmic balance, she supposed, but the truth is that Rhetta just stood there, slack jawed. Mr. Bates did lots of talking, and Vera Bates was the one who fell down, ripping clods of the mud and slamming them into the river water.

"How could you do this?" Vera's voice went hollow and throaty, like the bleat of a goat or an old woman's cough.

Rhetta wasn't sure who the words were meant for, but after Vera Bates said them, Rhetta turned. With the straightest shoulders she could manage, she ran back down the gravel path. She turned and ran as fast as she could to Nellie's house.

"Don't you cry, Rhetta." Nellie had whispered. "Don't you cry."

14

RHETTA REMEMBERS THE TOWN BOOGEYMAN.

When Rhetta Ballou took the off-ramp to Fort Angus, she smelled the Stewart-Rico paper mill first. It was not a strong smell, and she doubted any non-local would even know to smell for it. It was a subtle odor, part burning wood with a bit of sulfur, like lit matches or smoldering leaves. The smell came through an open car window just at the highway exit, and was over almost as soon as it appeared. For most travelers, if the smell was ever noticed, the conversation was quick:

"Is that the car?"

"Is what the car?"

"Oh, I guess it's nothing. I thought I smelled something."

For Rhetta, the odor made her shoulders tense and her jaw set.

Rhetta signaled right, and she thought about the arrest at the old river shack. Her mother would get the details later from the *Fort Angus Republican,* but last night she'd gotten them directly from her sister Christine, who'd met Wendy Jo's ambulance at the hospital.

The details were clear: Sam Shane was arrested at Leander's old place. Wendy Jo might die. Rhetta needed to come home. "And what about Emmett Pratt?" Rhetta had wondered later, but had not thought to ask.

In the midday sun, Rhetta saw the distinct rooflines of Fort Angus in the distance, and there were no evening shadows or holiday decorations to soften the details. As she drove into town, across the bridge and toward the square, the dormant lights of the theater marquee welcomed her. Although Leander was long dead, Rhetta remembered him well.

Leander had managed the Sunrise Cinema in Fort Angus. Leonard A. Lambert on his birth certificate, but "Leander" because of an uncanny resemblance to an obscure 1940s comic book character with the same name. He showed Rhetta the faded comic book once, laying it on the glass of the candy case, and she tried not to agree that yes, there was a clear resemblance to the drawing of the ugly boy and the caption, "a fat little nothing named Leander."

Squat and bald, with thick-rimmed, Army-issue eyeglasses, Leander was also slack-jawed and bow-legged. He wore old-man olive work pants and a pit-stained T-shirt.

Leander was not an attractive man, but when Rhetta met him, she was fourteen and begging for a job that wasn't in the potato fields.

"Do you have any experience with food service?" he asked.

She said no.

"Handling money?"

She told him she could learn.

One week later, Rhetta Ballou sat behind the concession stand of Aroostook County's oldest and longest-running movie theater. The original Sunrise was an old-fashioned, Depression-era film palace with plush seats and an ornate, wooden balcony. Leander hired Lamen Hollander to convert it from a single screen to a double screen by placing a pressboard wall straight down the center of the auditorium and rigging up a speaker system from spare parts he picked from the dump. With new plastic orange seats in the first six rows and the threadbare blue velvet seats in the back twelve rows, the interior was mismatched and architecturally jarring, but it was the only movie hall in all of Aroostook County, and after the conversion it was considered a legitimate multiplex.

Leander walked with a limp and drove through town in a tricked-out Army jeep. He hollered at children when their balls bounced into the street, forcing him to brake abruptly.

"Santa don't visit the graveyard!"

Mothers and fathers began to make their babies run inside when they saw Leander coming. "Fucking weirdo," the teenagers spat, after Leander kicked them out of the theater for making too much noise. "Fucking homo," the Angus, Compton, and Kinkead cousins yelled from their new cars as they shot the loop through town, angrily throwing fast-food wrappers and soda cans out the window.

Leander fed day-old popcorn to the pigeons that lived under the marquee, and it made him a prime target during those sweaty, early summer evenings. Rhetta would discover the sting of Fort Angus's unspoken rich–poor class system, but as the town boogey-man, Leander received amplified public disgust.

Most people did not know that in addition to theater management, Leander ran a small ammunition factory in the offices directly above the lobby, loading shells for himself and his hunting buddies. When the show started, he'd finish feeding the pigeons outside and retreat upstairs to the tiny airless room, making bullets until intermission. The dirty window of the ammo factory looked directly onto the town square, and after watching Leander get picked on night after night, Rhetta wondered if he ever thought of taking advantage of the quick, clear shots he had. She also wondered if the teenaged boys realized that for a supposed lunatic, Leander used amazing restraint.

On Saturdays, parents dropped off their little boys—shrieking, flatulent things—a half hour before the movie started. Leander leveled the little ones with a look, but he yelled at the older ones, physically pushing them from the theater and instructing Rhetta to call their homes.

The Angus and Compton and Kinkead parents, usually pissed and disbelieving, walked warily around Leander, unsure what he'd do next. Each would collect a child, either crying in a chair or waiting cross-armed outside. The parents entered the lobby quickly, nodded to Leander, and left without speaking.

It was common knowledge that Leander had a rundown clapboard camp on the edge of the muddy Abnaki River. This camp, Rhetta heard, was where he molested little boys, where he poached wild animals, where he killed people, and where he held orgies with men.

In truth, Rhetta knew it was where Leander cooked spaghetti sauce. He'd bring his late-summer tomatoes, spices, and plastic containers. She never asked him, but Rhetta always imagined he kept an old dial radio on the counter next to the kitchen sink, similar to the radio in the ammo factory. A static-filled radio plugging old-time gospel music in a tomato-scented kitchen instead of the dirty ammo factory was an image she liked better.

When Leander returned to work after hunting season, he always gave Rhetta a frozen quart-sized Tupperware bucket of spaghetti sauce.

"Tastes good on toast," he grunted.

And it did, Rhetta remembered.

As she drove into town, it all came back—the smell of Leander's ammo factory and the sound of wild little boys running the length of the concession stand.

It was Leander who gave Rhetta a ride to the Bangor clinic.

"You're a big girl, Rhetta." That was the extent of his conversation, but one night during intermission he pushed a pamphlet across the ticket stand. It was from the Aroostook County Health Clinic. Protect yourself, the words read.

She knew about birth control, but in Fort Angus it wasn't like she could just go to the clinic where Dr. Benis worked, and ask Rosemary Angus's mother for pills. Karen Angus was the staff nurse, and as soon as Rhetta left, she'd call up Phil Compton's mother and tell her to talk to Phil. Phil would deny being with Rhetta, and then the two ladies would speculate about who else it could be. Or, whose it could be.

All this, Rhetta ran through her mind as she lowered the radio volume, to explain how Leander drove her two hours down I-95 to Bangor in his Army Jeep for birth control pills, only to learn she was already pregnant.

"Can the clinic call you at home?" the receptionist asked. "Is it safe?" Rhetta said no, and then answered a list of other health questions. They made a strange couple, the bald, fat, ugly man sitting in the white plastic waiting-room chair and the teenage red-head standing straight-backed at the check-in table.

She'd asked them to do it right then, and they did.

The procedure itself was quick and painless, but as she lay in the dull gray recovery room with a half dozen other women, all focusing on not making eye contact, Rhetta knew she would take a long time to heal. She also knew, at that moment while feeling waxen and empty under the blinking fluorescent clinic lights, that she could no longer live in Fort Angus.

The heavy silence inside Rhetta's car was broken by her nervous giggle as the exact circumstances leading to her exit from Fort Angus came to mind. Not the abortion or the affair, but the day she told her mother she was leaving.

F-O-R-T A-N-G-U-S. These were the letters pinned onto the red spandex underpants of the junior varsity cheerleading squad the day Rhetta quit the team for good. When Rosemary Angus handed her the fuzzy white patch in the shape of a G, Rhetta folded her pleated skirt and told the coach she was out.

"Why did you do that?" Rhetta expected Ada to ask, calculating the cost of her cheerleading shoes in piecework at the factory. It wasn't her fault at all, Rhetta reasoned on the walk home, so Ada couldn't be too mad. In fact, her mother might even laugh. Rhetta and Wendy Jo tried out as a joke and made the team, owing largely to Wendy Jo's loud screaming voice. Neither girl could do a cartwheel, but the idea of tormenting Rosemary Angus for a full season was too much fun to resist. Unfortunately, Wendy Jo quit school before it got fun.

Rosemary was the one who assigned Rhetta the G. If she'd been given the F or the S or the N, Billy Rudnick would not have been inspired to call out what he did, and the remainder of the pep rally crowd would not have jumped on board. And, ultimately, Rhetta would not have been involved at all. As it turned out, she was the only one on the squad opposed to the cheer that ended with each girl flashing ass to the pep rally.

"No really. It'll go like this." Rosemary jerked out her hip, swung her upper body around until her hands touched the floor in front of her, and her rear end was pointed up at the bleachers. The idea was for the junior varsity team to do something outrageous. To show they could jump, dance, and wiggle with as much talent and enthusiasm as the prettier senior varsity squad.

The coach set Rhetta's folded skirt on the locker room bench, rallied her troops, and dismissed Rhetta with her hand. "We'll perform without her, girls." When Rhetta tried to say that the G was critical, the coach told her to go watch from the bleachers.

So Rhetta made her way to the edge of the crowd, still carrying her red and white pompoms. The voices of the students echoed in the large gymnasium, sounding louder and louder as they competed against the shrill resonance of the band tuning. The principal stood at the edge of the basketball court, laughing with the English teachers. The basketball coach opened the door of the boy's locker room slightly, the whistle around his neck shining in the amber lights. The varsity cheering squad was giggling on the sidelines, and two of the girls struggled with the painted paper hoop they'd devised for the boys to jump through.

Rhetta knew the schedule. The band would play "Louie, Louie," and the junior varsity team would do their dance routine. Then the band would ramp up, and the varsity cheerleaders would take the floor. When the players entered the court, the principal would announce their names and rev up the crowd to see the team outside and onto their waiting bus. The bus would drive to the next county, where the game would be played, and the rest of the school would be dismissed a half hour early.

From the safety of the crowd, Rhetta watched the routines as planned. The junior varsity team pranced from the sidelines into the middle of the gymnasium floor and forming a V, like a troop of weak and honking geese, they squawked out the cheer. It started soft and then drifted off as one by one, they bent over to show the crowd their rear ends.

The effort, however, was not as climactic as Rosemary had hoped. In fact, few people were paying attention. The teachers stood chatting at the end of each row, ensuring that everyone clapped politely.

Then Billy Rudnick saw that the letters on the asses of the junior varsity cheering squad, minus the G, actually spelled something worth shouting. When he stood up and began to cheer, "Fort Anus, Fort Anus," it sounded so much like "Fart Anus," that the crowd mimicked it as such.

It took the principal a moment to get the joke. Rhetta watched his mouth switch from a large smile at the audience participation, to an uneven and questioning smirk, eyes squinted toward the cheerleaders, and then into a round, horrified capital O.

By this time the energy in the bleachers had reached a fever pitch. "Fart Anus, Fart Anus," chanted the crowd. The band began to play unevenly as some of the instruments shook from stifled laughter.

Rosemary and her squad remained on the floor. Rhetta watched her count off the letters. When Rosemary realized her error, she covered her mouth with her hand and ran toward the locker room. The other girls, thinking this was part of the routine, ran after her, smiling big pep rally smiles.

The varsity cheerleaders looked back and forth between

their coach and the principal. Rhetta saw them whisper "what do we do?" All the while, the crowd continued to stomp and chant "Fart Anus."

Because Rhetta stood at the edge of the bleachers, she was close to the parking lot exit. She slipped through the heavy gymnasium doors, the early spring air a contrast to the sweaty loudness of the gym. The parking lot was full of cars, and the big team bus was parked perpendicular to them, blocking a row of at least a half dozen. Rhetta stuffed her pompoms into a stained metal garbage can, zipped her sweatshirt, and walked home.

That was the day, Rhetta remembered, that she walked home and took stock of her resources. She had close to $3,000 of theater money in the bank, and she'd just bought Wendy Jo's old Chevy hatchback. Rhetta was just sixteen when she told her mother she was leaving.

That day, instead of watching her new baby sleep in a laundry basket, Ada watched Rhetta stuff items into a little backpack of her own. Toothbrush, sweaters, books. Rhetta had no idea that her mother was thinking this scene was too familiar, that Ada remembered doing the same thing. Rhetta had no way of knowing that Ada was remembering her own teenage fight with Nellie the morning when she'd left, and that she heard Nellie's voice in her own mouth.

"You think there's something better out there? That what you think?"

Silent, Rhetta continued to pack with her head pointed

downward. When she said no, there was an edge in Rhetta's voice that Ada hated, like Rhetta thought she was stupid.

"You," Ada said, pulling Rhetta's chin up with her index finger. "You think you're better than us?"

Rhetta shook her head.

Ada's impulse was to slap her daughter, to slap her straight across her smart-talking mouth, and Ada remembered that was exactly what Nellie had done. When she had left Fort Angus, Nellie asked where she was going to go and who she thought she was.

And now, if Rhetta thought she was better than Ada, better than her whole family, then goddamned if Ada planned to let her turn into one of those stuck-up Anguses. Goddamn that.

"You," Ada said, resisting the urge to slap her daughter. "You," as she'd said many times before, "are the one who is going to drive me crazy."

Rhetta did not stop moving. "It isn't about you," she said softly. "It isn't about you."

What did that even mean, Ada wondered. It wasn't about her? It sure as goddamned hell was. Ada's breath got more and more pronounced when Rhetta said, "It's this program."

Rhetta rummaged under a pile of clothing on her bed and brought out the folder. "For smart kids."

Ada remembered Rhetta showing her something weeks before, something about moving away, and even though she heard the words, she never thought her daughter would follow through. A pre-college program for high school kids. They live in the dorms, and it's all paid for by the state.

Now it was all a panic again in Ada's mind, just like the day she'd brought Rhetta home, and every day since. She felt her thoughts spinning around like the hospital front door once again. Her daughter was leaving.

"Get out of this town," Ada whispered with resignation, sitting down on the edge of the bed. "Don't be like me." Rhetta stopped packing to watch her mother, now crumpled on the bed, and she clutched. Her instincts were split. Half of her wanted to run fast toward her car, and half of her wanted to throw down the backpack and run fast into Ada's arms.

Ada spoke louder, "Just get out of this town." She rose, straightened her back, and repeated as she closed the bedroom door behind Rhetta, "Don't be like me."

As the Sunrise Cinema got closer, Rhetta remembered even more details. Leander had died from diabetes complications a few years ago, and the theater had shut down. The *Republican* ran an obituary that Ada had sent her, but too late to attend any funeral service.

It looked like there was new management, though, as the marquee was now painted a bright green. The lights inside were on, too, and Rhetta wondered if the ammo factory still existed now that Leander was dead. She also wondered how Leander would have felt about last night's arrest at his old shack.

It was no secret that Leander's shack was a party spot, but a hideout for a killer? Rhetta did not believe Leander would have sanctioned that part. Not a single bit.

15

EMMETT PRATT CONTEMPLATES WOMEN.

$\mathcal{E}$mmett Pratt had financial means, but he lived alone in his trailer with no woman to share them. If any person in Fort Angus suspected Emmett was worth more than his mother's old trailer home and a secondhand pickup truck bought with cash from Drew Freid because his wife Joyce couldn't drive a stick, Emmett might have risen above suspicion in his Aunt Sheila's murder.

As it was, Emmett was considered a nice guy, but quiet. He pumped gas every day except Sunday at the Irving, and he ate most of his meals at the Miss Angus Diner.

The Miss Angus was famous throughout Aroostook County for its homemade "mile high" pie, and families drove from as far away as Millinocket to enjoy a piece served with vanilla-flavored whipped cream on top.

Sometimes for a change of scenery, Emmett drove ten miles across the border to eat at the New Brunswick Diner instead. Both restaurants were authentic old Worcester train cars, from when the Bangor & Aroostook Railroad stopped in Fort Angus every day at noon on its way to eastern Canada.

In its heyday, when lumber was king, northern Maine was the tenth-richest locale in the entire country, and Emmett thought about this as the chubby-faced waitress told him to take a seat anywhere he'd like.

The Miss Angus had an original wood interior, and the New Brunswick Diner was all chrome. Both places had bright neon signs in the window and table jukeboxes to flip while he waited for his food, a meat-loaf sandwich at the Miss Angus and the turkey special with poutine at the New Brunswick. Each order came with homemade white rolls and cold butter, the rolls at the Miss Angus made fresh by a group of ladies from the Fort Angus Imperial Baptist Sancturary.

Emmett always sat at the counter because the booths seemed too melancholy for one person alone, and while not exactly flirting, Emmett did his best to make conversation with the ladies waiting tables. The waitresses stood behind the counter, chatting among themselves as they finished their work, topping off ketchup bottles and refilling the salt shakers. The waitresses, for their part, were used to Emmett Pratt's presence after so many years.

In the beginning, when he was still a teenager, the waitresses would smile big and tease him with a wink. As they slid Emmett's order to the counter with manicured hands, they offered to head over to his house and cook for him personally, if he knew what they meant.

Although Emmett knew what the waitresses meant for sure, his face would color, and he spent supper time looking straight down at his stainless-steel fork, repeating a mantra, although he did not know that word, of chew, chew, swallow. Chew, chew, swallow.

When Emmett gave them no reaction, the waitresses assumed he must be shy, or a little bit slow, and they soon gave up. Emmett Pratt became just one more fixture to ignore. He overhead them talk of menstrual periods, abusive boyfriends, and recipes for rum drinks. He listened while the waitresses gave each other hugs, and again when they cursed "don't be such a fucking bitch." From his position at the counter, Emmett watched the waitresses interact, and it was from these waitresses that he formed his silent thoughts about women.

Over the years, women had been interested in Emmett because he filled his uniform shirt with lean muscles, and he walked standing tall. His smile was a small one, lopsided and sweet, and different women drove to the filling station every day for fuel. Emmett would walk out, wiping his hands on a rag, and the women would smile at Emmett as they rolled down the car window.

"Hey there," they'd say, and Emmett nodded, immediately second-guessing the nod and thinking he ought to have said something out loud like "hey" instead. His brother Johnny or his father Dexter would have thrown back a "hey yourself" and then looked at the women as if they were naked. They would have offered an easy grin and then said something like "you, in that short hair cut, are the most refreshing thing I've seen here all day."

Johnny or Dexter would hand a woman's change back through the car window, but they would not let go, prompting a playful tug of war on the dollar bill and a bold suggestion like "why don't you spend that money on drinks for us later on?"

Johnny or Dexter knew how to talk to women without shifting from leg to leg, sweating through an undershirt, and wanting to run away in the exact opposite direction.

His inability to talk confidently with Fort Angus women would have been more of a problem if Emmett was actually interested in any of them. Emmett liked women, in theory, but Fort Angus women fell into three categories for him.

He watched the thick, bland, mouse-haired women who were loyal to the Fort Angus IBS. These were the Fort Angus good girls. They wore plaid skirts and loose dresses all year long. These women clutched at their Diet Pepsi bottles when they pulled into the station for a fill-up, unsure of how to operate the pump and relying on Emmett to care for them. While not ugly, these church women washed into the background with muted conversations and a false sense of adventure.

"Can you just imagine what I thought? Can you just imagine how I felt?" They talked to each other with energy when they thought Emmett wasn't listening. He watched them giggle, back from a ceramics or quilting class. Emmett noticed they all drove automatics. They talked about diary entries and chocolate recipes for when they felt like being bad. They talked like a chorus of fat little squirrels about other people's lives and other people's adventures. "Can you just imagine doing that?"

Once, Emmett overheard a back and forth about a cousin going all the way with her boyfriend. What it felt like, what exactly happened. He remembered the shocked expression on the girl's pale face, her jaw losing all muscle as it dropped. The woman was almost in tears, talking about salvation, yet she told the story with such a level of interested detail that Emmett suspected the story had been told many, many times before.

Although any of these women would have been glad for a young man like Emmett with a full-time job and an itinerant soul to save, Emmett openly cringed when he thought of listening to "can you just imagine, can you just imagine" year after year in his own home.

On the other end of the spectrum, Emmett watched the Fort Angus bad girls sashay past the Irving in short shorts, heavy with eye makeup and leaning over whatever beater car was idling in the municipal parking lot. He watched those girls walk the length of town each Saturday night, lingering from car to car as if they were shopping for goods in a discount store.

Emmett noticed a new crop of these girls each summer after the carnies left town. During the Fourth of July celebration, the traveling midway would set up on the fairgrounds. A dozen rickety rides and two rows of games would blink with bright yellow lights as the carnival workers stood by in coveralls or grimy tank tops. These carnies had a talent for spotting teenage girls who had never been noticed before.

"Hey beautiful," they'd holler, looking straight at girls who were not, technically speaking, beautiful. The not-so-beautiful girls would stand a little taller for a moment, and when that new high of admiration set in, Emmett noticed the girls made a point of strutting up and down the rows of carnival workers all night long, giggling and daring each other to go say hello.

When the carnival broke down for the season, there was a void, and Emmett watched these girls, now used to feeling sexy, try to fill it by taking their newly noticed selves downtown. While Emmett appreciated the jiggle of tits walking in high-heels, these girls were not for him. Pretty and willing, yes, but Emmett did not want to worry that his own admiration would never be enough. He did not want his woman to enjoy being hollered at by carnies.

That left the third category of Fort Angus women, and for Emmett, these were the ones who got away. The bank teller, for instance. Cindy was her name, and Emmett remembered how his pillowcase smelled like her vanilla lotion for weeks after she left town.

The ones who got away drove into the Irving, their cars overloaded with college supplies. This happened mostly in late August or early September. Emmett watched them drive down the Main Street, signal toward the interstate, and disappear. He filled gas tanks when these girls were home for vacations and then as they turned into women, for family weddings and funerals, but Emmett knew they were lost forever. He was thinking about these women because it was now past Labor Day.

It was well after Labor Day, in fact, and his aunt's killer had just been arrested in a bizarre raid the night before. Emmett was relieved. He had intended to fire Sam Shane for stealing from the petty cash anyway, but now Emmett was spared the task. He was still sorting out how he felt about Sam coming into work each day even after he'd killed Sheila for her prescription drugs. Emmett thought that part was especially cold, the coming back to work part, especially given how every person in Fort Angus believed Emmett had some part in the crime, and Sam himself had kept that talk going. Sam worked at the shop for nearly two months after he'd done the murder, and Emmett never even suspected as much.

Emmett thought about his mixed emotions as he closed the hood of Lyddy Compton's Buick and took the money from her hand on the morning after the arrest. Even though Sam had been arrested, Lyddy Compton would still not make eye contact, so Emmett turned to watch Nevie Shane strutting down Main Street with her little sister. Emmett noticed Nevie's ridiculous red cowboy boots and short shorts right away, as did the pit crew from behind the annex. Nevie ignored the whistles and pulled her sister's arm tighter as she moved past the open bays.

Emmett watched down the road and wondered where she was headed. It was early for a movie, and school was out for the potato harvest. When the guys in the garage got too loud, Emmett walked around the corner. The men, a half dozen in Carhart pants, stood at the door, watching the disappearing figures of Nevie and Jincy Shane.

"You all finished for the day?" Emmett asked this rhetorically, as he nodded toward the two cars still up on lifts and waiting to be serviced. When the men turned back to the jobs at hand, Emmett wiped his hands on a rag from his back pocket and told the cashier he was taking a late lunch.

Emmett's dog Lucy barely moved when he put the key into the ignition. In fact, she rolled her old yellow belly just enough so Emmett could fit in the cab, but when she saw that it was no trick, and the truck was actually moving, she sat up, rigid with unexpected excitement.

When Emmett's truck pulled beside Nevie and Jincy Shane, Emmett noticed the practiced way Nevie approached the passenger side. Her thin arms swung open the door, and she smiled when she hopped into the cab. He asked where they were going and nodded at the irony when Nevie said nowhere.

"I like your dog," Jincy said when Emmett pushed Lucy to the floorboard. As Jincy scratched the dog's ears, Lucy's eyes shut and her head rested on Jincy's lap.

Emmett told the girls he'd seen them walking, and he'd heard the shop guys hollering. When he told Nevie he didn't like that, Nevie rolled her eyes and told Emmett that she appreciated his concern, but she could totally handle it.

It was the way Nevie said she could handle it, emphasizing "totally," that made Emmett sigh. Nevie Shane was smart, he knew that. His Aunt Sheila said as much about both Peg's girls, and it was a tribute or act of kindness toward his aunt that made him concerned enough to offer them a ride.

He watched Nevie pull down the sun visor. She puckered her lips, scrunched her freckly nose, and applied shiny lip gloss from a pink plastic tube. Emmett noticed that Nevie Shane was beautiful. Jincy, too.

As much as Emmett hated to see the good ones go, he did not want Peg's girls stuck in Fort Angus. He did not want to see Nevie get pregnant, and then spend her life chasing down some man for child support. He did not want her to fade away as a cashier at the grocery store or as a crude-talking diner waitress.

But Emmett had no words for them. There was nothing he could form in his mouth that meant don't sell yourself at such a low price. He had no words for "not this," or "make a plan for yourself," so when Nevie Shane arched up her eyebrows in the visor mirror and told Emmett to mind his own business, his own shoulders dropped. He never was good at talking, especially to women, and even more especially to young teenage women.

Instead of giving life advice, he asked if they were hungry, suspecting the answer was yes. When they nodded, he offered to take them to the Miss Angus Diner. Over cheeseburgers at a booth, Emmett asked the girls what they wanted to do when they finished high school.

"A veterinarian," Jincy answered quickly, while Nevie chewed on a potato chip. Nevie told him graduation was so far away, she had plenty of time to figure it out.

16

MILES COMPTON WITNESSES THE CONFESSION.

After Miles Compton was told again, politely but firmly, by the head of the Fort Angus Facility for the Elderly that, no, his volunteer services were not needed, he found his father's room at the very end of the dementia corridor and said good-bye for the evening. Across the hall was Nellie Ballou's room, and when Miles walked past, Nellie shot him a wink from her open door. His father failed to recognize Miles, so he folded up the day's newspaper and placed it on top of the bedside table.

Miles had no particular intent that night as he walked the three miles from the eldercare facility to his mother's house by way of the Abnaki shoreline. His father was now officially committed, he was rejected from volunteering in any official capacity, and the night, like all nights, stretched out long and empty.

Summer had moved into late September, but the air remained thick and warm. The sky was clear, and Miles halfheartedly spotted constellations as he sidestepped the trail behind the nursing home. The footpath was overgrown, tucked in between the remnants of a prickly old raspberry bush, and it led down to the gravelly riverbank. It was a shortcut, of sorts, and Miles walked carefully to avoid wetting his shoes.

He ducked his head around and under the lower hanging branches. Above, he watched the skyline of Fort Angus, with its radio tower light glowing red in the distance.

"Rudolph," he remembered his mother saying one Christmas Eve, when the family drove home from the church service. "That must be Rudolph," she said, pointing up to the blinking light in the distance. Miles believed her for a moment until a much older Phil smacked his head and told him not to be so stupid.

Rudolph is what Miles remembered on his nighttime walk along the river. He was not concerned about anything beyond how he should spend the rest of his life, and more immediately, how to avoid getting his shoes muddy or wet.

Miles later told Officer Monroe that he couldn't explain why he took the river path home that night. Or, more importantly, why, when he saw the old cabin lit up in the distance, he changed direction and crept toward the angry voices.

"Because you're a pervert," Officer Monroe thought, but did not say. "And that," he thought in his head, "is what perverts do."

The voices were agitated, Miles told him. A man, and then a woman. He heard a slap. They were arguing, Miles said.

It was a shadowy walk, and Miles straightened his back at every twig snap and branch rustle. The shack in the clearing was lit, and Miles wondered briefly how they got electricity run so far down to this end of the river, but his thoughts halted when he saw two people in the glow of the old kitchen window.

"Did you do this to Sheila?" A young woman Miles recognized as a Delfino had slumped into a kitchen chair. She put her head in her hands and said for the man to tell her he didn't do this. She said it over and over, as her fingers combed her blonde hair and her elbows braced her shaking head.

"Wendy Jo," the man said. "Wendy Jo, listen."

Wendy Jo Delfino? Miles thought, and then remembered her married name was Pratt. He squinted to make out the features. Sure enough, that was Wendy Jo. Wendy Jo had once babysat Miles, and her daughter, one of the babies in the Delfino family, had been in his graduating class. He remembered walking the stage in a black cap and gown, directly behind Wendy Jo's daughter. He remembered this because when she was handed her diploma, she looked left at the audience and winked. Then a whole section of the bleachers stood up and cheered. In contrast, when Miles took his diploma, there was only subdued, polite clapping. Miles remembered that tinny, weak sound of his parents' applause against the bleachers full of Delfinos.

And this was Wendy Jo? Miles saw the Delfino blond hair, and the tiny Ballou build, but he would never have recognized her as his former babysitter. When she spoke, she showed graying teeth and while no Delfino had ever been fat, there were now no curves to her body at all. She wore a green tube top, and Miles could count her vertebrae when she bent forward.

For a moment, Miles considered calling out. "Hey, Wendy Jo, remember me?" but he stopped short when the man pulled her chin up in his hand.

This was when Miles recognized the man, his back no longer to the window, as the same man who had changed his mother's oil at the Irving annex. He recognized Sam Shane's thin mouth, with his lips stretched back like an animal.

Sam Shane pulled Wendy Jo's chin up quickly with the side of his thumb, but he did not speak. He just grinned and nodded. Then he said that sometimes you've got to do what you've got to do.

Sam Shane dropped Wendy Jo's chin, and Miles could hear her sniffles through the window. He stood up, pushed the metal chair away from the table, and moved toward the cupboards. He pulled down a dozen boxes of sinus medicine, some peroxide bottles, and carefully set them on the old Formica table.

Miles had no personal experience with methamphetamine, but he vaguely recognized the process from an old public television news program about the state of drug use in rural America, and at that exact moment, he realized he'd seen something big.

Big, big.

The only Sheila in town was Sheila Hollander, who'd been killed, and Miles connected the dots. He thought quickly of leaving. He imagined slipping quietly backward through the woods, back along the silvery shore to the little bedroom in his mother's home and forgetting that he'd ever seen Wendy Jo.

Then, just as quickly, he imagined himself busting into Leander Lambert's old river shack, delivering a roundhouse kick to Sam's jaw, and grabbing Wendy Jo by the hand. He liked to imagine himself a hero, and wondered if a hero's action would erase his presence on the state website.

But instead, Miles took one breath and then another. Despite running scenarios in his head, Miles Compton felt in his pocket for his cell phone, noted the time, and then moved quietly back in the direction he'd come. He moved quietly to avoid detection, but Sam was so concentrated on his project, he would not have noticed. Wendy Jo, strung out and exhausted, moved from the meth shop in the kitchen to try sleeping on Leander Lambert's old iron bed.

When Miles had backtracked up the hill and once again through the scratchy old raspberry thicket, he held out his phone. Instead of walking into the Fort Angus Police Department, Miles called in a tip to the state trooper line.

Yes, he asked to remain anonymous. He remained anonymous for about an hour, while he watched the old river access road from a distance, pacing through the trees and expecting to see a line of squad cars, lights flashing, en route. Or a stealth operation, with unmarked vehicles and men in body armor and dark baseball caps. Miles wondered how the state police would take Sam Shane into custody, but he never wondered if they would actually show up. He had just heard a man confess to murder, and murder was a big deal, so as each minute passed, his adrenaline levels dipped and spiked. "What," he thought, "could be the hold up?"

Eventually, fearing for Wendy Jo's physical safety, he walked with his hands stuffed into his pockets the mile into town and toward the brick police station. The police station was attached to the county jail, and the cell windows made a row of dim little squares. Miles could see figures walking back and forth across the plastic panes.

It was past suppertime, and Officer Monroe sat alone at his desk, watching a black-and-white antenna television hooked up to a dusty VCR.

"Yes?" Officer Monroe looked up when he saw Miles Compton standing in the paneled lobby.

Miles started with his long walk along the river. Then he spoke about the meth supplies, and how he saw Sam Shane nod and admit doing something bad to Sheila Hollander, but Officer Monroe waited until Miles said that he'd called in the tip to the state police to stand up. He opened the door separating the lobby from the office and gestured for Miles to enter.

It took all the strength Officer Monroe had inside his narrow brain to proceed on this information from Miles Compton, but since Miles had already called the state guys, he had no other option.

There was no avoiding some level of action, and the state guys would be expecting follow up. They wouldn't understand how it was just a matter of time before Officer Monroe got Emmett Pratt to confess. They'd want to know what Officer Monroe was doing that night, and there would be the hassle of paperwork, too. Since Miles had called those state guys first, Officer Monroe was going to miss the Chuck Norris marathon on the station television.

Officer Monroe considered all this information, and telephoned the sheriff's office for assistance, but he made no mention of Miles Compton. He figured, and Miles understood, the credibility factor of a pervert was suspect at best.

Miles Compton remained anonymous, and Sam Shane was arrested late that night for intent to distribute. Then, the state guys found the prescription bottles with Sheila Hollander's name still on the label, all stacked up on the top shelf, just beside the kitchen radio. After they found those bottles, Sam was charged with her murder, too.

It turned out, according to Lyddy Compton's *Fort Angus Republican* that week, Sam Shane had kept the actual killing knife, and the State of Maine had a fancy crime lab that picked up some of Sheila Hollander's exact blood. Lyddy was shocked to read the last part, thinking "why in the world would you hang onto a murder weapon?"

Lyddy was also shocked when they officially let Emmett Pratt loose from suspicion. She knew about the commotion down at the river the night before because she'd heard it directly from the pastor. Or rather, she'd been filing paperwork at the church office that morning when Christine Delfino came in for emergency pastoral counseling with the reverend. Christine had not shut the office door completely, and her voice carried easily to Lyddy's ears.

"Well, I'm still not convinced," Karen Angus said, as the two women signed a greeting and prayer card for Christine. "Emmett must have been involved somehow for Hartley to be so convinced."

Lyddy nodded, not questioning Hartley Monroe's judgment for an instant. He'd been smart enough to figure out the real killer and brave enough to go down to the old river shack in the middle of the night. Hartley, she'd begun to call him by his first name, was a smart man, and if he suspected Emmett Pratt had something to do with the crime, it was not her place to doubt him

Hartley Monroe had been over to Lyddy Compton's house twice for coffee since the mayor started living at the nursing home. He nodded to Miles each time he opened the door, wondering how in the world a woman as special as Lyddy could have raised such a pervert.

For her part, Lyddy was pleased that Miles did not unnerve Hartley. She knew she was the subject of some gossip for these coffee mornings, but part of her liked this type of talk. In fact, she telephoned Karen after Hartley had left. "Can you just imagine what I was thinking? Hartley Monroe just turning up on my porch like that? Can you just imagine?"

17

Emmett Pratt's parents reconcile.

*D*exter Pratt leaned against Lora's dusty convertible on the day his son Emmett was officially released from suspicion in Sheila Hollander's murder. Sam Shane had been arrested the night before, but Dexter did not know any of this. He only knew it was well after Labor Day, but the morning was still a hot one. He spat into a plastic Mountain Dew soda bottle with an inch of brown liquid already at the bottom while he waited for Lora to come to the door of the trailer. It was now close to lunchtime, and he'd been waiting outside since before breakfast.

Lora had woken up early, realized the mistake she'd made with inviting Dexter into her bed, and she kicked him shirtless into the driveway. She'd told him to get his shit and get out. She told him the things she'd not been able to tell him all those years ago when he'd been sitting in jail for running off with skinny Lyddy Compton. Lora told him he was a lying, cheating sonuvabitch, and she said to get the hell out of her bed right now.

Lora said all this only a few moments after she'd woken up curled naked into Dexter's chest. His chest hair, now gray, felt soft against Lora's back. Dexter had gently removed her wig, the brown one, the night before, and said he liked her short hair best. He said he liked the way it showed off her big smile. Dexter said her one tit was gorgeous, and that he'd never seen a woman with only one tit up close. He traced her scar with his calloused thumb and told her she looked fierce. "Fierce" was exactly the word he used, so Lora felt fierce for the first time since she'd gotten sick.

Dexter told her she was always the one lady for him, and the only thing he ever done right was marry her and make their boys. And after all the good stuff in between, they fell asleep together in Lora's old waterbed for the first time in more than two decades.

"Morning, Dad" Emmett had said as he passed his father in the driveway. Officer Monroe had called him into the station early, which was strange because it was several weeks after Sheila's murder, and Officer Monroe was still the one who came to Emmett, not the other way around. Emmett expected Officer Monroe's car in the driveway, but he did not expect a 7 a.m. telephone call from Joyce Freid requesting his presence in town, and he was not sure if this was good news or bad.

Emmett slipped his wallet into his back pocket and ran fingers through his wet hair. He opened the truck cab for Lucy to jump up, and he was so anxious about the call to the police department that he got to the very end of the Hope Station turnout before he thought to wonder why his father was in the driveway without a shirt.

Thinking back, he'd seen two places set up at the kitchen table with a package of bacon on the counter and coffee in the perco-lator. Since his mother didn't cook, and his father loved bacon, an image of his father and mother having breakfast together moved through his brain, but Emmett immediately shook it out as impossible.

He resolved to deal with whatever his parents were fighting over when he got home, and as he pulled into the police station, he hoped that Officer Monroe would get his questions finished quickly.

Standing shirtless in the driveway, Dexter Pratt had no idea his son was about to be officially dismissed as a suspect in Sheila Hollander's murder. With an apology, even. He had no idea the night before, when he'd seen Lora at the grocery store and offered to buy her a milkshake, just like the time he'd first taken her out as a teenager, that Sam Shane would be arrested at the old river shack.

When he saw Lora standing in the bread aisle with her left hip cocked out to the side and supporting the blue grocery basket, Dexter was struck by how little she had changed. Each detail, from her fancy red shoes to her long, polished fingernails was the same as he remembered.

And that ass, he noticed. His ex-wife had an ass that wouldn't quit, so for old time's sake, he snuck up behind her, pinched her bottom and said it again, just like when they were in high school. "Hey pretty girl, can I buy you some fries to go with that shake?"

Lora remembered, too, just after she shrieked, dropped her basket and whipped around to find her ex-husband's hand still on her shorts pocket. Her first instinct was to punch his face, but that instinct quickly moved to a little nostalgia because Dexter Pratt in his late fifties looked good.

She hadn't expected Dexter to age well because in every one of her fantasies he died from crippling disfigurement. But, standing there in front of her, Dexter in his fifties looked as good to her as Dexter in his teens.

And, as her ex-husband stood in the grocery store aisle wearing a clean white T-shirt with a six pack of Coors dangling from his right hand and grinning down at her like some flirty village idiot, Lora figured the least of what he owed her was a meal. She told him he better have money because she was going to buy the most expensive item on the menu board.

When they'd finished their supper at the Miss Angus Diner, and Dexter paid cash for her plate of fried clams, she took him back to the trailer, and Dexter was happy. He was happy enough to wake up early and get to fixing breakfast for them in the kitchen. He'd started the coffee in a dusty percolator that had been a wedding gift years prior, and he'd found a frying pan at the exact moment the telephone rang. He moved to lift the receiver, but he heard Emmett grab a phone down the hall and say, "That's fine, Joyce. Just let me take a shower first."

When the bathroom door closed and the water turned on, Dexter returned to Lora's bed, snuggling in for another round. Lora Pratt, for her part, saw the situation a little differently in the light of morning and ran him back down the hall whispering the longest string of curse words she knew. Her bathrobe hung open, and her stance was wide as she pointed up at Dexter.

"You kiss people with that nasty mouth?" Dexter grinned, leaning in toward her. Lora slapped his face and told him to get his cocksucking ass out of her house. She threw last night's boots into the dooryard while Emmett's dog whined and paced between them. Whispering so Emmett wouldn't hear, Lora told Dexter he was the most sorry, useless, worthless man she'd ever seen and he had some nerve seducing her like that, as she slammed the trailer door and turned the deadbolt with a satisfying clank.

This was how Dexter happened to greet his son in the driveway. Had Dexter not decided to run to the grocery store for a six pack the night before, and then buy Lora supper, he may have seen the commotion at the river himself.

Six state agents entered Leander Lambert's old shack, and they took Sam Shane on the spot. Wendy Jo was lifted pale and jittery into an ambulance. The agents seized the methamphetamine supplies as evidence, as well as the bottles of painkillers with Sheila Hollander's name on the label. The agents did all this with blue lights flashing far enough through the dark so several of the assisted-living-facility nursing staff stood outside with arms crossed, wondering what in the world was going on.

When Emmett returned to the trailer that evening after work, the same day Hartley Monroe had done his best impression of an apology, his mother's car was gone from the driveway, and none of her clothes were in her bedroom. Emmett expected this, though, because he'd gone straight to work from the police station that morning, and he'd gassed up the convertible for Lora late in the afternoon.

It was a strange day, and he ended it by tossing the day's mail onto the kitchen counter beside the dirty frying pan, soaked with water and cold bacon grease. Sam Shane was now arrested, and Emmett had been officially released.

It should have surprised him to see his father sprawled in the passenger seat beside his mother with an old duffel packed up in the back. On this particular day though, Emmett figured anything was possible, and as he looked from one grinning parent to another, he wondered how Dexter had managed to talk himself into Lora's car. He wondered, but did not ask. His parents smiled and snuggled into each other, and Emmett just grinned back and told them he'd do his best to make it south for Christmas. He was thinking, he said, that he might like to see Florida this year.

Lora got out of the car and hugged her youngest son good-bye, telling him she'd wire up some money to help get him through. Emmett knew this was a well-intended lie, but when he hugged his mother, he realized just how long it had been since he'd had a woman in his arms. Emmett Pratt resolved to make some other changes in his life, too.

As it happened, once Emmett left the trailer park to find Officer Monroe that morning, Lora had watched Dexter from between the curtains. The curtains, she'd noticed, were the same ones she'd sewn with Sheila when they'd bought the trailer lots side by side. Dexter had carried Lora over their first rotten front steps like some fool in a movie back then, but now he sat on the neat doorstep. He'd put his boots on, but he had no shirt.

Dexter sat on her doorstep, spitting into that soda bottle all morning. As Lora took a shower and then ironed her clothes for the day, she noticed the plates set on the table and the bacon on the counter. She turned on the television to watch Philip Spalding return from the dead on *Guiding Light* with a million items running fast through her head, the quickest being what in the world she was going to do with a half-naked ex-husband sitting outside her door.

Sheila was buried, Odie wasn't her problem, and her own boys were settled into Fort Angus with families, or in Emmett's case, a job. Although her cancer was in remission, Lora liked being near the doctors in Florida. She liked having the public beach just a few miles away, too. Lora had moved all those years before on a whim, running away in a fit of anger that still simmered, but Tampa felt more like home than northern Maine. She had good neighbors in the condo development, and she worked decent hours at the Kroger. The oranges in Florida were better than any she'd ever tasted in Maine, and she liked how people were not afraid to paint their homes in vibrant shades of salmon and turquoise, two of her favorite colors.

She paced the length of the trailer, noting the home her son had made. The towels, old but clean, were folded on a shelf. The bathroom was tidy, and there was no dust in the hallway. Lora understood Emmett in some ways more than his brother Johnny, and she defended his living alone for so long.

"No, he ain't gay," she'd say, absolutely offended. "And he ain't retarded either." Lora knew her son was just quiet. She knew he was a thinker and liked time to himself.

Lora padded back and forth, straightening a picture or touching a coat as she wondered what to do next. She wanted to go home, but as she ticked off the things in her mind that felt like home, she came to the conclusion that Fort Angus was no longer her home.

Lora hated to think as much, but she supposed Dexter was a little bit responsible for that. She peeked at him through the window again, still sitting shirtless on the steps, until Emmett called with the good news of his release.

After Emmett called, she stopped peeking at Dexter through the window, got dressed, and tossed Dexter his shirt on her way to the car. She told him to get in, but to leave that stank-ass spit bottle in the trash.

She drove to the police station, left Dexter in the waiting car, and waved hello to Joyce at the front desk. She found Hartley Monroe bent over the old time clock, fiddling with a broken piece of metal. In an effort to get his attention, Lora poked him in the back with a shiny red fingernail.

"I told you Emmett ain't the killing type."

When Officer Monroe turned around, Lora poked him again in the shoulder, and then a third time. As he stuttered for a response, Lora Pratt turned and walked back toward the door.

Her high-heeled sandals made a clicking sound on the tile, and Officer Monroe watched her tight ass move in little denim shorts. Despite just being poked, he could not help thinking that Lora Pratt was still a sexy, sexy woman.

While Lora was busy poking Officer Monroe, Dexter waited in the car. He relaxed into the front seat, testing out the radio scanner. As he waited, he watched a familiar figure walk the length of sidewalk in front of the courthouse, and when he recognized her, he blew an involuntary whistle.

Carrying a hot coffee and sandwich meant for Officer Monroe, Lyddy Compton stood tall in her new dress, and as Dexter recognized her, he felt a wicked desire to take advantage of Lora's car with the key still in its ignition. He figured they could be over the state line before Officer Monroe knew which direction they'd chosen.

Given that the mayor was now in the nursing home and out of his mind, Dexter weighed his options and thought quickly. It never occurred to him that Lyddy might not have him, because when she heard his whistle she looked up to meet his eyes.

Unfortunately for Lyddy, that gaze was interrupted by Lora Pratt's shriek as she exited down the police station steps. She had pushed open the door and spotted Lyddy Compton walking straight toward Dexter.

Lyddy heard Lora holler "oh hell, no," and felt something crack against her head. On instinct, Lora had reached down and thrown her high-heeled sandal at Lyddy's face. When she saw that she'd missed, she threw her second shoe, this time connecting squarely on Lyddy's forehead.

Lyddy spun from the blow and tried to make sense of what just happened. She'd been smacked in the head by Lora Pratt's sandal, and she flipped through her brain for any sort of correct and polite response.

Lora, now barefoot, hopped into the car and slammed into reverse. She hollered, "Yeah, that's right," over her shoulder while Dexter put his hand over his mouth, trying not to laugh.

As Lora drove down Main Street, she set her jaw and focused on the road. Since Sheila was buried and her baby was no longer in trouble, Lora figured that she'd pack up and get back to Florida by the next day or so.

And somehow, after the night they'd just shared, and their boys all grown up, and the fear in Dexter's wide eyes when she threw her shoes at Lyddy Compton, she figured maybe there were some things she needed to work out with her ex-husband, too.

This morning she had worn no wig, just a brightly colored scarf of Sheila's tied around her natural hair. When she reached the trailer lot, Lora told Dexter he might as well come inside and cook the bacon before it spoiled.

18

ODIE HOLLANDER BEGINS TO FEEL BETTER.

*S*am Shane's bloodied face cost Odie Hollander an extra two weeks in jail and another full year's probation, but Odie didn't protest. Not one bit.

Breakfast was finished, and he watched Spick get processed through the dirty window of the community room. From his stance, leaning against the metal door and smoking the last of the two cartons his mother had given him, Odie had a clear sightline straight down the fluorescent hallway. He watched Spick's wiry, twitching frame as he got issued his orange jumpsuit. He watched Spick get handcuffed once again, and then he watched the guard lead Spick closer down the dull mint-colored floor.

Odie figured Spick would be at county lockup until the state filed official charges. Then, when the evidence came in and the doctor assessed his threat level, they'd sort out where to have the trial. This, Odie thought, could take days, or weeks.

As he projected timelines in his head, Odie also counted the forty-five minutes it took to fill out Spick's paperwork, take the photos, and get all his supplies issued. Even though breakfast was finished for the day and Odie watched the cook bag up two pieces of toast and a cup of coffee for Spick to eat in the processing room, Odie knew Spick would eat other meals with him. Odie's knuckles cracked almost involuntarily with anticipation, excited about this opportunity.

Odie Hollander meant to take his time. He listed ideas in his head, like bashing Spick's face down against a cafeteria table, or punching that sweet spot near his kidneys to make him shit himself before he dropped to the ground where Odie would then kick Spick's jaw. He thought about doing Spick in with a knife to his chest, and then across his neck the exact way Spick had done his mother.

He spent a great deal of time contemplating all the ways he'd break Spick's body, but when the metal door unlocked and Spick was led to the community room, animal instinct kicked in. Odie just leaped and started punching.

Sam Shane, skinnier and shorter than Odie, crumpled like an old oil rag. He curled up underneath Odie's bulky frame, and it took a radio call to the front room to get Odie's fists untangled from Sam Shane's face. Odie pounded his fists all over Spick until two more guards put him back into his cell and then removed Sam to another part of the building.

When Odie saw Peg in the visiting room, she was not impressed. "Baby, he's family. And we don't know anything for sure."

Odie did not respond, but instead fixed on Peg Shane's freckled face. He watched every flicker and eye movement with interest and intensity. He watched Peg's hands fish into her purse for a lighter, and then offer him a fresh pack.

He later read about Spick's arrest in the *Fort Angus Republican*. He read about the bust, and all the details leading up to the bust, to include a quote from Hartley Monroe. "We have brought the perpetrator to justice."

There was a photo of a smiling Officer Monroe in front of an old Formica table topped with meth cooking supplies, some baggies of weed, his mother's prescription bottles, and a pile of cash. Officer Monroe was leaning on the table in the photo, and Odie remembered the many times he'd sat at that same table. When Leander was alive, Odie and the boys at the shop used to beg Leander for his gin.

Leander would share, and the lot of them would drink until they puked, rallying just enough to find their way back home. "Keep it between the trees," Leander would say, passing out face down on that old kitchen table. "Keep it between the trees, boys."

From the article, Odie gathered that somebody called in a tip about Spick's meth kitchen at the shack, and then a bunch of state guys stormed in and arrested him. He read that Wendy Jo was in a detox program, and that her kidneys were so bad, she might not make it. At the end of the article, the Imperial Baptist Sanctuary requested prayer-shield volunteers.

The newspaper writer tried to make the story look dramatic, like a cop show, but Odie knew Spick. He guessed there was no struggle at all, and no "armed standoff" for sure because Wendy

Jo was there, and she would have been too strung out to resist anything, which Odie knew from personal experience. He figured Wendy Jo passed out on the bed or on the couch somewhere, maybe after whining for Spick to get her a blanket.

And Spick. Spick was a weaselly little fucker, and he would have run, not fought back. Odie noticed the newspaper said the shack had a stockpile of weapons, but Odie also noticed that no mention was made of Spick actually using those weapons. Yes, Odie thought, Spick probably had a gun or two stashed in the old broom closet, but if Spick was high, he would have hidden. If he was clean, he would have run.

As it turned out, Odie was correct on all counts, and Sam Shane was apprehended in a rusty shower stall, where he'd squatted when he heard the door bust in. He'd been taking a piss, saw the reflection of the blue lights through the shack's little window, and quietly stepped into the shower, pulling the curtain across. Since he had a jackknife on his belt, he was considered armed.

Odie read all these details in the paper, but he read them after he had already, technically, assaulted Spick on that first morning. The paper came out each Wednesday, and Spick was booked early on a Monday. He had spent several hours that Sunday night in the police cell being questioned before he was brought upstairs to the official lockup.

When Odie first saw Spick at the jailhouse, it was a surprise. Odie had taken to smoking by the community room window so he could watch the downtown traffic. Fort Angus offered one major intersection with a single traffic light, and Odie passed the time by watching the cars drive. The jail was situated on a corner of the four-way stop, the post office on the opposite side. A bank and the newspaper office stood on the remaining corners.

Sometimes Peg took Jody-Ray to the post office, and when she did, she'd wave at the jail. She couldn't see all the way inside, of course, but she told Odie that she liked to think he could watch her like that, caring for him out in the open.

On the night of Sam's arrest, Odie had also seen Miles Compton walk up the police station steps, framed in the amber exterior lights, and he wondered why Miles needed the police. He ran down a few scenarios, but none of them rang true in his head. It was too late for Joyce Freid to process a speeding ticket, as Odie had watched her walk out the door at five o'clock on Friday and cross the street to where Drew Freid waited in his truck. Odie watched Joyce lean over the seat and kiss Drew's cheek.

Since people just called if something was stolen, Odie figured Miles wasn't there to report a theft either. Miles was walking unescorted, so it couldn't have anything to do with the pervert website. It had to be something important, Odie reasoned, given that it couldn't wait until a weekday morning.

This was how he figured out that Miles Compton had something to do with Spick's arrest. He wasn't one hundred percent sure until he read the anonymous tip part in the newspaper later that week, but after Miles came to the station that night, it was the only thing that made sense.

Odie got a cramp in his neck from looking out the window on the night of Spick's arrest. After Miles left the building, he watched Officer Monroe and a carful of staties transport Spick, handcuffed, in cutoff jeans and an old T-shirt, from a squad car, up the steps, and inside the building.

Odie rubbed his neck muscles and pondered the realities of Miles Compton having something, maybe everything, to do with the arrest. This meant Odie now owed a favor to the town homo. He didn't know what, or how, to think.

Peg repeated that she was not impressed, and then changed the subject. She'd been picked up as a field boss for the Angus potato farm. It was easier, she said, than working on the harvester. She put her girls and Jody-Ray into the field, too, and was hoping the harvest money would take care of Christmas.

"I want the kids to have a nice Christmas," she told Odie.

She asked Odie if he was coming home to her, or if he was moving into Sheila's trailer when he got released, but Odie just shrugged. Peg kept chattering about Christmas presents, but Odie could not concentrate. He saw her lips moving and her hands gesturing, at one point rubbing her belly where the new baby was growing, but Odie just saw and heard static.

Spick Shane had killed his mother, and Peg Shane was carrying his baby again. He had less than three months of confinement left, and he owed a favor to the town pervert. Those thoughts circled around his brain in coils while Peg counted out a roll of singles and pushed them across the table. "For the vending machine."

19

Rhetta and Emmett Pratt shake hands.

*E*mmett recognized Rhetta Ballou immediately when she drove into the Irving for gas. When she got out of the car and extended her hand toward him, he shook it, the whole time feeling awkward, thinking that her handshake was such a formal thing. Rhetta immediately regretted the handshake, too, hearing Ada's voice in her head telling her not to act better than anyone, but it was done, and there she was, shaking hands with Emmett Pratt at the gas station on a late September morning.

When the handshake broke, Rhetta wanted to tell Emmett she was glad the whole mess got sorted out with his aunt's murder. She wanted to tell him that she'd followed the details in the paper, and that not for an instant had she believed he had anything to do with the crime. She wanted to say thank you for that silent walk twenty years ago and for being her friend in the potato fields. Rhetta wanted to say all these things, but she was standing in a little rain puddle, and the words would not form.

"Good to see you, Emmett," she finally spoke, hoping she sounded genuine. Emmett shifted from one foot to the other. "Good to see you too, Rhetta," he nodded.

She asked for some fuel, but did not get back into the car. While Emmett pumped for her, she studied him. His shirt was clean, and so were his pants, save for a tiny oil smear near his front pocket. He held the gas pump with calloused hands and balanced a toothpick in his mouth. Apart from some wrinkles around his eyes, Emmett Pratt at thirty five looked very much like the Emmett Pratt of fifteen.

Rhetta wondered about the forces that conspired to keep him here at this same gas station for the past twenty years, the same forces that conspired to push her out of Aroostook County and away from Fort Angus. They'd both grown up poor, both quit the mess that was high school, and they'd both managed ruined small-town reputations.

As Rhetta thought about these things, Emmett was thinking similar thoughts. He knew she was on her way into town, because her suitcase was leaning against the backseat. It looked like she had packed up some toys and coloring books for the little cousins, too. He guessed she'd be staying for a visit, and decades-old details overtook his brain.

In the far corner of what used to be defense barracks, there is a large plaque, noting the history of Fort Angus.

Emmett had seen this tarnished plaque his whole life and knew the story it told of Colonel Angus and the young Micmac's offer to show him good land, but he didn't think it went down like that, and he had asked Rhetta as much on the night they sat together as teenagers at the old barracks on the hill.

"I suppose you're right," he remembered her saying as she traced the raised letters of the story with her left hand. They'd walked all the way up the garrison hill, Rhetta in bare feet while Emmett carried her shoes. They were the first words spoken in an hour.

He watched her features, and without knowing he was actually seeing, he let his mind catalog every detail. Her red hair was pulling from its braid, and bits of dried flower petal kept falling when she moved. The straps of her pink bridesmaid dress slipped off her tiny freckled shoulders, and she bunched up the bulky skirt with a fist when she walked.

He wanted to tell her that he loved her, that he would love her forever, but he was just fifteen, and he did not know it yet. Emmett wanted to grab Rhetta's hand and pull her tight into his chest. He wanted to tell her that he'd protect her with his life. Emmett Pratt wanted Rhetta Ballou to know that she was the most beautiful person in the world.

"Want a smoke?" These were the words that came from his mouth as he dug into the pocket of his denim jacket and extended the pack toward a young Rhetta.

Rhetta drew her hand away from the plaque and looked over her shoulder at Emmett. She nodded, accepting a lit cigarette, and when she first placed it to her lips, she smelled the spearmint gum that Emmett had been chewing. They sat on a picnic bench and watched the lights of Fort Angus down the hill while Emmett wished he could stop time.

"I think they're all full of shit." These words from Rhetta startled Emmett, and he sat up. She stared straight down the hill, her thumb fumbling with her other fingers. Emmett nodded.

She had said "shit" on the exhale, and her shoulders dropped. She repeated herself, as she hugged her knees into her chest.

"I need to get out of here."

Emmett heard her words, but they sounded like empty little echoes. He did not doubt Rhetta Ballou, but he wondered where she'd go. Her family was in Fort Angus, and had been for generations. The Ballous were, as far as Emmett was concerned, as deeply rooted and fixed to the town as any of the Angus and Compton and Kinkead families.

Nellie Ballou, Rhetta's grandmother, was the town bad girl back in the days when there were soldiers on the border. At least, that's the way Emmett had heard it. It might not be the best family history, but he reasoned it was a hell of a lot more interesting than the other town family stories. Her mother Ada worked at the glove factory, and her aunt Joyce just got hired as a secretary at the jailhouse. Rhetta's aunt Christine was mother to Wendy Jo, who Emmett's brother was going with.

If Emmett had the words at fifteen, he would have told Rhetta that she was sewn into the fabric of Fort Angus, and if she left, she'd leave a jagged and frayed tear. Besides, he thought, nobody leaves Fort Angus. And then instantly, he corrected himself, nobody leaves Fort Angus and ever comes back.

The thought of Rhetta Ballou leaving and never returning, gave Emmett gooseflesh, and Rhetta noticed his shiver. "You getting cold?"

This is what Emmett was thinking while he dawdled at the gas pump with Rhetta. Like that night in the park, he wished he could stop time. Rhetta's hair, shorter now, hung forward and hid her face until she brushed it behind her ear, carelessly, with a single, casual motion. It was as if he could scratch the surface of something bigger in his brain when he stood next to Rhetta Ballou, but before he had time to work it out, the pump clicked off, and he was telling her what to pay.

After Rhetta left, Emmett regretted not buying her gas. He wanted to give her something, a present, anything to make her think of him. She paid Emmett with cash in her wallet, and she mentioned the arrest one more time. "So there was an anonymous tip?" When she saw his embarrassed face, she regretted the mention.

He nodded, and they were both acutely aware of the irony. It took the word of one anonymous caller to release Emmett Pratt from suspicion. As a Pratt in Fort Angus, his own word was not, would never be, good enough.

"Do you have any idea who it was?" The words felt alien in Rhetta's mouth, but she could not stop them. Twenty years prior, she could share a silence. Now, so far removed from her hometown, she struggled to fill the space between them.

Emmett shook his head again.

Some man had called in a tip that Sam Shane was the person who murdered Sheila Hollander, and that he was living in Leander's old clapboard shack down at the edge of the river. This man had heard, Emmett said, Sam Shane bragging about it to a woman who turned out to be Wendy Jo. This man saw Sam with a weapon, too.

So when Officer Monroe investigated, along with some state police, they found Sam Shane in the shack with a nearly unconscious Wendy Jo.

As the state guys processed the shack, Officer Monroe rummaged around in an old freezer. "What in the world would anybody do with so much spaghetti sauce," he wondered as he moved the long-frozen plastic containers into the sink.

Rhetta later saw the photos in the newspaper and recognized Leander's old Tupperware in the background. Emmett saw the same photos in the same newspaper and recognized his dead cousin Lamen's old gun lying on the table in the background.

Emmett and Rhetta had both tried to work out who had called in the tip, who would care enough, and who would be in the loop.

Emmett first thought of his cousin Odie, but he was still in county lockup. Peg Shane, Sam's sister, wouldn't rat out family, and the paper said the caller was a man. His father came briefly to mind, but Emmett reasoned that his father was somewhere en route to Florida right now, preparing to set up house with his mother.

Rhetta suspected one of Wendy Jo's brothers, but she could not imagine any of them with enough ambition or desire to make a call. Her stepfather Clint flashed across her brain, but even if Ada begged him to, Rhetta knew he would not get involved. No, even with a day to think about it, neither Emmett nor Rhetta could summon up a realistic vision of who would be interested enough to care.

In her rearview mirror, she watched Emmett Pratt walk from the pumps to the garage annex. The drive through town toward Ada and Clint's house took all of two minutes. "Blink and you'll miss it," was the clichéd old joke. Joyce, on her lunch break, waved from the courthouse steps and Rhetta honked the horn as she drove by.

The road wound through town and up the hill, and Rhetta slowed the car and made an abrupt left down the old Bluebell and drove for five miles until she hit gravel. There, on either side, were John Rainier's potato fields. The twenty or so field workers —mostly children—were on a lunch break. They seemed tiny, shoulder high to the potato barrels, eating their sandwiches and drinking directly from jugs of purple Kool-Aid.

Rhetta pulled her car into the grass and watched the group, all in dirty T-shirts. She watched for ten minutes or so as they finished eating their lunches. One of them ran to the woods clutching a wad of toilet paper while a large boy stood up and began to pummel a smaller blond boy. Another boy with a ball cap intervened.

Rhetta leaned against the car and ticked the children in the field off by their biggest features, easily seeing the Delfino blonde hair and the Shane freckles. She looked for the Kinkead pink cheeks. She focused on the biggest, sturdiest young men on the digger truck, sorting out the Compton from the Angus, as one final memory smashed into her head.

It was a week after the potato harvest ended, and the fourth-grade desks were bare plastic squares. Colored corduroy pants and barrettes with braided ribbon were fashion standards, and Rhetta owned neither. Fads were a waste, Ada said, and she was busy with the baby and her factory job, so Rhetta brushed her own hair straight every morning. She bent over *The Little Princess* that day, struggling with Sara Crewe's unfair position in literature, watching Rosemary Angus move her long braids side to side across her desk.

Rosemary sat in front of Rhetta, and her corduroy wale made an engine sound when she twisted in her seat. Her two best friends sat on either side, and Rosemary had to turn quickly to keep up their conversation. Left and right, the strawberry-blond braids slid across the desk, and Rhetta removed the piece of gum she'd been hiding in the far recesses of her mouth. While she was imagining Rosemary's hair covered in gum, as well as a long-lost soldier father arriving to claim Rhetta as his princess, Phil Compton was gearing up. Phil had hatched a bunch of garter snakes, and he kept them in an aquarium by his bed. He'd brought the snakes to class for Science Day, and the aquarium sat on a table in the back corner all morning.

The teacher ordered the class to read quietly while he stepped next door, so when Rhetta felt that cold wiggling on her neck, instead of shrieking, she just whipped around and punched Phil Compton square in the balls.

She stood up on reflex, delivered the punch, and then snatched the snake from his hand as he dropped. On instinct, she threw the snake hard against the wall. The snake, brown and innocent, touched her hand for just a second before it sailed over Rosemary's head in an uneven arc, slapping against the chalkboard, and then falling lifeless onto the orange carpet.

"You killed my snake," Phil wheezed from his kneeling position. All the teachers loved Phil's dimples. All the girls, too. Phil went to the same church as Rosemary, and he was cousins with all the Kinkeads. Because of this, Rosemary stood up beside him.

"You killed Phil's snake," she screamed.

By this time, half the class stood over Phil and half the class moved to the spot where the snake lay on the carpet. Billy Rudnick began to jump, and the girls next to him, too, when he said "There's blood!"

Hearing the word "blood" from his classroom, the teacher returned and looked from Phil to Rhetta to the snake in the corner, which Billy Rudnick was poking with a pencil.

Actually, that part was completely made up. Not the braids or the corduroys or Rosemary or Phil. Or even the snakes. Phil Compton did bring snakes to the fourth grade class, and he did put one against Rhetta's neck, but she didn't punch him in the balls or kill the snake.

Rhetta wished she had though, so while she watched the field workers eat their lunch, she remembered it that way first. She wanted it to have happened that way, and, sometimes, she even told it that way. She wished more than anything that she could step back in time to make it happen that way, so she could tell her cousin Wendy Jo and her mother Ada. She wanted most of all to tell Nellie, who would laugh.

But, the truth is that Rhetta just sat there at her desk. When she felt Phil's snake, all cold and sliding along her hairline, Rhetta just held onto her book and started to cry. Phil laughed out loud and Rosemary called her the biggest baby she'd ever seen.

When the teacher returned, he sent Rhetta to the bathroom to wash her face, and as she shut the classroom door, she heard him yell. He yelled about respecting personal space, and fears, and the worst, about sensitive people.

When Rhetta walked back in, every kid was on their best behavior, staring forward. Rosemary's braids no longer sprawled on the edge of Rhetta's desk; they were now tucked neatly on her shoulders.

Any one of Rhetta's cousins or aunts or uncles would've smashed a fist into Phil's crotch without even thinking, would've boasted to the teacher that they'd do it again. Wendy Jo would've spit, too. And when they got home, Nellie would ask to hear the story again and say the Comptons were all a bunch of little assholes anyway, so good for showing them you wouldn't take their shit.

"Don't take any shit," Ada would repeat. "You're just as good as anybody else."

Rhetta shook that scene from her head, righted her posture, and thought that she'd remembered enough for one day. She watched the dynamics of the potato fields—dirty-faced children playing, running, working. She watched the field boss, it looked like Peg Shane, a short freckled woman, blow her whistle and herd the kids back to task. Peg Shane handed one of the girls a jug of water, and as Rhetta recognized the shared features, she realized it was Peg's youngest daughter. Rhetta calculated quickly, figuring Peg was about her own age, and Rhetta tried to imagine herself as a mother to two teenagers.

She watched Peg blow a whistle to signal that lunch was over. Peg herded all the children back in place, evenly spaced across the potato-field rows, and Rhetta stepped out of the car and leaned against the door.

Peg's daughter, named something funny, Rhetta remembered reading in the newspaper, was digging her row methodically, dropping potatoes into her basket and then walking the basket to the barrel. She didn't look up, at least not that Rhetta could see, but Rhetta knew she was watching.

Rhetta could feel the gritty dust in the girl's gloves and the mud on her neck. She felt the shared ache of one basket, then another, and another until the day was night. Knowing this, Rhetta also knew that no distraction went unnoticed, so when the Shane girl stopped picking for a moment and turned to face the road, Rhetta waved. Embarrassed, the girl's head went down again, and like that handshake with Emmett Pratt at the gas station, Rhetta immediately regretted the gesture.

She regretted the wave because to the Shane girl it was a foreign act, initiated by someone who did not know the rules. Rhetta meant the wave as an act of acknowledgement, a small move toward reclamation of her place that said, among other things, "I understand," but with the Shane girl's ducked head, Rhetta realized her mistake. No county girl would openly connect with a stranger, and Rhetta knew that to the Shane girl wearing dirty gloves Rhetta was a stranger, and with a quick gesture of her palm, she'd exposed the girl's uncomfortable vulnerability. Her instincts were off, and Rhetta reminded herself to get them in check before she arrived at Ada's house. It took all of five minutes to physically leave Fort Angus as a teenager, but she felt it might take an entire lifetime to find her way back. As Rhetta steered her car from the overgrown edge of John Rainier's potato field and back down the old Bluebell road, she remembered her own days in the potato fields with its exhaustion and sweat and rote motion of bending and picking and thinking of nothing.

The details of one particular day in those fields made her shut her eyes with discomfort because, as she moved to adjust the radio volume, Rhetta looked down at her sleeve and noticed that she was, without intention, wearing a red coat.

The End

Acknowledgements

Many thanks, first and foremost, to my family. My mother, Betty, assured me that if any person attempted to draw false parallels between our real lives and the words contained in this book, she'd say flat-out that she didn't know what I was talking about, and I was always a liar anyway. "Fiction writer," I corrected, and she said it was the same thing. I agreed with her assessment.

I owe much to her, and I hope she knows how limitless my love is for her. She is a good woman and a good mother.

Many thanks to the American Association of University Women for the Bennington College fellowship that eased my transition from "grant writer" to "book writer." Many thanks also to the Maine Writers & Publishers Alliance, its members, and its Board of Trustees. Thanks to Sven Birkerts and Bob Shacochis—two of the finest prose teachers, and Robert Vilas for teaching in a more abstract way.

I must also note contributions from the following, my earliest readers: Joan Dempsey, Jessica A.T. Gilpatrick, Josephina Gasca, and James Hayman. My later readers, too, added a special blend of support and daily encouragement: Anne Mommsen, Amy Lindner, Kimberly Nelson, and Ruth Mann Smith. And, of course, the giants upon whose proverbial shoulders I stand: Hannah Holmes, Joyce Maynard, Elizabeth Peavey, Bill Roorbach, and Suzanne Strempek Shea.

Thanks to Beth and Todd Wagstaff, who quietly asked about this book during Trav's performance—Todd's question meant the world to me at the time, and I'm not sure I ever told him so. Thanks also to my daily readers: Agustina, Carla, Cynthia, Heather, Jamie, Jill, Kelly, Laurie, Marie, Maya, and Ruthie. Erin Irish needs thanking, too, although I disregarded every one of her editorial suggestions. Thanks to Ralph Sordyl for offering the tour muscle, and thanks to Carson Lynch, Linda Bennett, Mary Herman, and Angus King for providing the physical space to write or edit much of this book. Add in Beth Ahlgren, who took that first writing class beside me so many years ago, and I am blessed with the best of all possible friends.

I owe an ocean of debt to my literary agent, Diane Freed, at Fine Print Literary Management, for seeing potential in my characters, and a separate ocean of debt to Michael Steere at Down East Books for bringing those characters home.

But mostly I need to thank my family again, both the big version and the small. The maternal side alone numbers more than fifty. Add my stepdad, Jeff, with his large family and the equally long list of Humphrey in-laws to the mix, and that's a lot of people to claim in a tiny space. Specific family thanks, though, to Kris Anne, Ben, and my niece Blythe. Tim and Dorene, too, as it was on their couch that this book was conceived.

At the other end of the state exists the smaller part of my family: Dad, Ann, and their quiet home. Douglas, too. Thank you for providing that essential balance.

My family, like me and like this book—like everything—are stunning with imperfection, and I love us for it. I could not imagine a better circumstance or finer group of people.

And finally, Travis. Always Travis, for being both the man of my dreams and the man of my reality—I love you.